Buckshot Ridge

Clint's only wish is to transform the Delta Ranch where he lives into a home, so that he can settle down peacefully with his wife-to-be, Belle Camden.

All is going smoothly until Clint witnesses a brutal murder. The killer tries to lie his way out of it, but Clint is not the lying type. When threats don't work, the killer takes Belle hostage. All Clint must do is admit he's made a mistake – forget what he's seen, move on – and his fiancée will be returned to him unharmed.

In a situation that goes against Clint's every moral code, in the end the choice can only be decided by gunsmoke – and blood.

Buckshot Ridge

Jake Douglas

A Black Horse Western

ROBERT HALE · LONDON

ISBN 978-0-7198-1650-5

Robert Hale Limited
Clerkenwell House
Clerkenwell Green
London EC1R 0HT

www.halebooks.com

Typeset by
Derek Doyle & Associates, Shaw Heath
Printed and bound in Great Britain by
CPI Antony Rowe, Chippenham and Eastbourne

CHAPTER 1

SUNDOWN

The first time Clint Reid came to the notice of the law was when he won the big poker hand, playing against the saloon's tinhorn gambler, Slip Riley, in Benson, Missouri.

The game was five-card Mexican stud – or 'flip' stud as it came to be named a little later on. The first two cards were dealt face down, the other three face up. The player could keep one of the first two as his upcard – or both if he felt lucky, placing his bet according to the card's value – high card high bet, low card low bet.

It could be a long or a short game; the latter, called 'sudden death', sometimes too appropriately named.

The house gambler kept them entertained as they played, reciting a long and mostly boring story about twin sisters who hoodwinked a rich beau and made their fortunes.

Clint Reid, in his late twenties and a sometime riverboat gambler, had heard the story before and knew it was one favoured by professional card-sharps who threw in lots of off-colour jokes, provoking laughter, sometimes prolonged – giving the story-teller cover to manipulate his cards.

Then Clint checked his hand and – surprise, surprise – found he had a winner, so he called the play, spread the pasteboards across the green felt cloth.

A bearded – and smelly – trapper on his left whistled through the only two teeth he had left in the front of his mouth.

'Hey, mister! You gonna have me runnin' round with the seat hangin' outta my pants. You could break the bank on that hand.'

'Yeah! Read 'em and weep, gents,' Clint said elatedly.

The others murmured too, and the gambler's long face became even longer. But when he saw Clint staring at him, he merely shrugged, planted a false smile on his suddenly dry lips, and tossed in his hand, saying as he leaned across to rake in the other players' discarded hands:

'You clean me, boy! First time in ten years, but I guess you've earned your two thousand.'

Reid tensed, saw the other gamblers moving their gazes towards him. '*Two* thousand? More like *four*, maybe five. Not sure just how much is in the pot.'

'Closer to five,' spoke up the Texan on Clint's left, and another man said, in clipped tones:

'I'd favour five.'

'Aw, now come on, gents,' the gambler said, sweat on his upper lip now, his smile only just holding. 'Our friend here didn't up his ante when he played his upcards like you're s'posed to. So that keeps the pot for this hand *down* to a lower level. Call it two and a half, to be generous, eh?'

'I'd call it something different,' Clint Reid said flatly, sensing the other players were with him. 'I – upped – my – ante.'

His cool grey eyes bored into the gambler's. The house man was losing his confidence rapidly as he shook his head and began poking among the discards.

'Aw, now, friend, don't let's have any unpleasantness. See? Here's your discards and your ten of hearts and six of clubs, but your other card, the queen of clubs, is somewhere in the throwaway pile. That's the one you should've called to up your ante. If you got rid of it, without doin' that – and you *did*—'

He stopped speaking abruptly as Clint Reid stood suddenly, the backs of his legs knocking over his chair with a clatter. 'Mister, that card was in with my other discards, where I put it.'

'No, no, *amigo*. I'm sorry, but you must've aimed wrong, dropped it in with the throwaways instead—'

'*Or*,' Reid cut in, his eyes narrowed, 'you flipped it across to the throwouts while you were rambling on with that long, boring story as a diversion.'

'Easy, man,' said the middle-aged pastrycook across from Clint. 'Don't let it get outta hand, now.'

7

The other players had their hands on the arms of their chairs, ready to throw them aside and duck as the gambler straightened, his face rigid.

'Your mouth's runnin' off, friend. I'd go easy, was I you. Hey! What the hell!'

He tried to jump back, but Reid caught the sleeve of his coat and jerked him halfway across the table, hands spread. Under his right hand, just showing, was the half-palmed queen of clubs, caught up on the sleeve's edge, ready to be dropped where the gambler wanted.

'You got sticky fingers, *friend*,' gritted Reid as the others vacated the table in a hurry. He brought his six-gun up in a blur of speed, rapidly reversing the hold and smashing the butt down on the gambler's outspread right hand.

The man screamed as bones broke in the back of his hand and in two of his fingers. He collapsed across the table, his weight tipping it over, spilling cards and money and the gambler himself to the floor.

The saloon was in uproar, men shouting and jostling to see what was happening, some running for the doors, sure there would be gunplay now.

Then a man wearing a sheriff's star thrust his way roughly through to the front and brought up a sawn-off shotgun, pointing it at Clint Reid.

'Drop the gun, feller,' he said, reaonably enough. 'Then we'll set us down and talk this over. OK?'

Reid placed his gun on the next card table, now emptied of players, and lifted his hands halfway to his shoulders.

'We got us a tinhorn here, Sheriff,' he said quietly. 'Palmin' cards and cheatin' me outta my winnings.'

The gambler was sitting down morosely amongst the scattered cards and broken glasses, holding his mangled hand against his chest as he rocked back and forth, uttering broken, whining sounds. The lawman lifted his gaze from him and looked squarely at Clint Reid.

'We'll all go down to my office. Won't be the first complaint I've had about Slip Riley here, but it'll be the last in this town.' He swung his cold gaze to Clint. 'You'll be on your way, too, before sundown. He goes north, you head south.'

'Hell! I'm the one was being flimflammed.'

'First and last time in this town, feller. Be gone by sundown.' The sheriff gave the shotgun a little jerk. 'You're lucky Riley's on my blacklist, but you'd be smart to take notice of my friend here.' He jigged the shotgun a little. 'He's got a big mouth – in fact two, *and he understands what I say.*'

'Sundown?' Clint nodded again. 'OK. But I'd rather go north than south.'

The sheriff looked at him, deadpan, held the bleak stare for a long minute. 'You like pushin' things, don't you.'

'Not 'specially, I but I don't like bein' the one getting pushed.'

'Better watch it. That mouth of yours can get you in a lotta trouble.'

' 'Specially if the law's doin' the pushin', eh?'

9

'Couple more words and you won't leave town for three months. You'll be lookin' at it through the bars of my cellblock.'

Reid started to speak, changed his mind and nodded resignedly. Then, just as the sheriff began to relax, he added, quietly, 'Still prefer to go north.'

'Goddamn!' was all the lawman said – and only just managed to refrain from squeezing the shotgun's trigger.

The sheriff wasn't as grumpy as he made out.

He not only granted Clint Reid's request to go north, but escorted him for several miles, stopping on a high ridge that looked out towards the twisting majesty of the Missouri River, and, beyond, to the distant, hazy Ozarks.

'You'd be wise to get that poker money into a bank.'

'Already have. Transferred it to Laramie through the bank here. Won't see a cent of it till I get there, but it'll be waiting for me.

'Mmmm. Not just a hothead, after all, are you? Well, dunno why, but I wish you luck.'

'Thanks.' Reid proferred his right hand but the lawman just looked at him.

'Gotta tell you, son, you're trouble, just goin' someplace to happen. But, 'long as it ain't around here I guess that's OK.'

Clint smiled thinly and touched two fingers to the brim of his weathered hat.

'Not me, Sheriff. I'm just headed for the quiet life

of a rancher now I've got me a stake. Might even send you a postcard when I get settled.'

'Don't get much mail, but I'll keep an eye out for it. Till I get tired of waitin'.'

Reid grinned. 'Er – no trouble over that gambler?'

'Riley?' The sheriff shook his head briefly. 'Been a pain in the butt for a long time. Kinda been hopin' someone'd shoot him. He's mean, so watch your backtrail.'

Clint touched his hat again, gathered his gear and they went their separate ways.

For no real reason Clint Reid decided to work out of Laramie, Wyoming. He didn't have any friends there, but during his wanderings he had heard of one or two acquaintances who had settled up that way and found decent lives for themselves and their new families.

Of course, that was some time ago and they might not even still be around, but it didn't matter. He had money in the bank, earning something called 'interest' without him having to lift a finger to earn even one extra dollar.

'Sounds good,' he'd told the bank manager who tried to explain it to him. 'Makes me feel kinda . . . lazy, though.'

Maybe it did, but, sure enough, the interest accrued while he looked around for somewhere to build the small ranch he had dreamt of for years.

The thing that made it a mite unreal was that he'd never played Mexican poker before, yet he'd come

11

away from his first game with what to him – a lone-wolf drifter – was a small fortune.

Well, the knew better than to look a gift horse in the mouth, and he set about building a new life.

He picked out forty acres on the slopes of a row of hills called locally the Deltas; his ridge was known as Buckshot Ridge. It was watered by two creeks that formed a kind of inverted V at their confluence. There was prove-up land available and he thought of apply-ing, saving his winnings and letting more interest accrue while he developed the land, but truth was, he didn't want any timetables to keep to; he was impatient to get his spread up and running, in this way, in his time.

He felt that now was the time in his life to settle. His wandering days were past, time to put down some roots. Make a future for himself and enjoy doing it.

So he spent a couple of thousand dollars of his winnings, made himself a tidy little ranch on the hill-side above the delta between the creeks, where grass grew belly-deep, and set about building up his herds.

Laramie was the nearest big town for that area, but there was a smaller settlement developing, which someone wihout much imagination had called 'Delta Creek'.

He got into the habit of ordering his needs from the larger stores in Laramie and having them shipped by wagon to Delta Creek, where he picked them up and took them back to his ranch. His brand was, of course, a triangle with a 'C' and 'R' within the lines.

'Not too much imagination there, either,' he told himself wryly, 'but I'll know any cow wearin' that brand is mine – and mine alone.'

Hiring a couple of men when he needed assistance, he made surprisingly good progress. He resisted the temptation to expand too early, although he missed some mighty good land going cheap, and concentrated on making his small profits: 'black' looked a lot better in his tally books than 'red', he figured.

Of course, sometimes he *didn't* make a profit and that frightened him a little: the way those times ate into his money.

He liked working alone, knowing he was his own boss, building some kind of future here, be it large or small. He even found time occasionally to visit the dances and barbecues the local population arranged every few weeks.

And there he met Belle Camden.

It was at a dance and he had asked her to partner him in a cow-country version of something called a 'waltz' in the hired hall, stressing that he was very much a learner and he hoped she was wearing substantial shoes.

At her puzzled look, he added: 'For when I stomp on 'em.'

She laughed. 'Oh, you shouldn't take such a negative attitude. You feel very lithe in my arms, and move fluently. You'll manage very well, I think.'

And under her tuition he did pick up the rhythm and managed to glide and slide around the dance

13

floor, with her feeling mighty light and *good* in his arms.

It wasn't long before they were seeing each other for rides in the country and she came and cooked for him a few times, leaving mouth-watering dishes for him to reheat and have at his leisure.

She was auburn-haired, was about his own age and, later, when she knew him better, admitted she had been engaged to marry a man two years previously, who had turned out to be already married and who managed to wheedle quite a deal of money out of her – until her big brother, Mitch, had discovered it. He had beaten the man to a pulp, then tossed him in the back of a telegraph wagon on its way to the wild country, where they were bound to run into Indians.

'My own stupid fault,' she admitted readily. 'I'm not what you might call – experienced – in the ways of courting and there are many things I do with more enthusiasm than is, perhaps, wise, and it carries over into relationships.'

'Seems all right to me,' he ventured. She suddenly looked at him in surprise and put up a dainty hand to cover her mouth.

'Goodness! What – what am I telling you all this for?'

'Must be because you're enthusiastic about me. You . . . think. . . ?'

He said it lightly but he saw by the fading of her faint smile that she knew he meant it, and that it was true.

They were betrothed, if not 'officially', and certainly not publicly, but there was an unspoken agreement between them that they would – eventually – marry.

He didn't neglect the ranch.

He bought some heifers to help improve the bloodline of his small herds, and built a fenced enclosure around an area at the base of the biggest mountain, where graze and water were easy for them to reach.

But there came heavy rains and a few boulders slipped down the slopes, flattening the fence that ran along the base of the mountain.

Naturally, the herds scattered, including the new heifers. But with the help of Belle's brother, Mitch, and a couple of his ranch hands, they recovered most of the heifers and other cattle.

There was a particular heifer that Clint liked, a kind of buckskin colour with a white flare beneath the right eye that made it look as if it was winking at any observer.

'I want that damn animal back,' he said. 'It' a one-of-its-kind and I – I like the way it plays and—'

'Oh, you're just a big kid at heart,' Belle chided him, laughing with that tinkling sound he enjoyed. 'It'll turn up eventually, see if I'm not right.'

But the presence of wolves bothered him and – as she had known he would do all along – he packed a warbag, tied it behind his saddle and rode out to find that damn heifer.

And that was when the law took a whole new interest in Clinton Reid, of Delta Ranch, Wyoming Territory.

CHAPTER 2

WITNESS

If some friendly Cheyenne Indians on the Great Plains, where he was hunting buffalo at the time, hadn't taken to him and shown him many ways to track – both animals and man – Clint Reid would likely not have even got within spitting distance of the heifer.

But he had learned well, found tiny tufts of that giveaway pale hide on bushes and scraped against rocks; they led him on a few false trails, but, finally, allowed him an actual sighting of his quarry.

It was up in the western end of the hills – a lot further from his ranch than he would have thought possible for the young cow to travel in the time – and it led him down a steep trail that zigzagged many times, which was lucky for the heifer. He saw where it had actually jumped across from one 'zig' to the next 'zag' instead of following the longer and safer

17

winding trail.

'Damn animal's part acrobat,' he allowed, tying his mount's reins to a bush and taking his rifle from the sheath before attempting the precarious descent. His six-gun rig was in his saddle-bags, but he didn't take it with him now.

Halfway down, his movements having started a small avalanche of gravel, he glimpsed the heifer. There it was below, contentedly chomping on sweet grass, too intent on eating to pause and see what had caused the pouring of a small stream of gravel over the nearby edge.

Of course, as soon as Clint began to descend it lifted its head, saw him and took off with a bound and a series of twisting movements through the brush. He lost sight of the animal within seconds.

'Damn!' he swore as he slipped, banged his elbow hard on a rock and dropped the rifle. It clattered, as it fell to the bottom of the rugged descent, making even more noise and no doubt driving the heifer to greater speed.

He had to work his way down, hanging from the edge of one high bend, then taking a risk and dropping on to the lower bend. He sprawled a couple of times, losing some skin from his hands before he thought to pull on his work gloves.

By that time he couldn't even hear the sounds of the heifer's passage; it certainly was nowhere in sight.

So, surprisng himself with the variety and intensity of the curses that spilled from his drawn-back lips, he made his clumsy way down – and came to a dead end.

At least, the trail ended abruptly and, unless he could sprout wings and fly, he had nowhere to go but back up and try to find another way down.

He was halfway to where he could now see he had missed the real trail he wanted, when he heard the first gunshot. He dropped flat instinctively.

It was a six-gun; it made that flat, dull-heavy sound of a hammer striking wood. He almost overbalanced and fell off the edge, grabbing a protruding rock that was set solid enough in the earth to support the strain he put upon it.

Raking his gaze around, hoping to spot the heifer, if not whoever had fired the gun, he saw a man running through the bush some thirty feet below – a hatless man with fear on his face, long unkempt black hair flapping around his shoulders. His clothes were well worn and ragged, tearing more as the bushes snagged them when he started to climb frantically, slipping and sliding but forcing his way onward. Something flashed on one desperately clawing hand: a ring, probably.

This was a man running for his life.

His face was contorted, spittle flew from his open mouth as he floundered on. He stumbled when the gun thudded again – two shots this time. He went down on hands and knees, spilling untidily, and stayed there, either hurt or winded.

Clint almost called out but he heard the sounds of the pursuer as he tore at the bushes and staggered into the section of trail where the downed man was now struggling to get to his feet.

19

'At – last, you – bastard!' gasped the man with the gun. He was wide-shouldered, and his hat hung down his back by its tie-thong, revealing thick brown hair that, despite being so unkempt, still showed traces of a natural wave.

Clinging to his shaky position, Clint felt an involuntary tightening of his gut as the big man stood above his exhausted and now cowering quarry. The man on the ground threw his arms across his face as the other lifted his Colt and coldly shot him three times, twice in the body – either bullet would have been fatal, Clint reckoned – and the third shot through the head.

Now that is one dead man! Clint thought, already crouching and trying to back up the path, hoping the killer wouldn't look up and see him.

The man was shucking out the empty cartridge cases from the smoking Colt and Clint did a quick calculation: he'd *heard* three shots and then the killer had fired three bullets into his quarry. So the gun was empty right now, but would be reloaded in a minute when the killer took fresh cartridges from his belt.

'Time to be somewhere else,' Clint murmured, already backing up, still holding the protruding rock for steadiness.

But his full weight had been on it for some minutes now, and suddenly it broke out of the bank. Earth and stones fell and pattered and, just to make things complete, he inadvertently gave a yell as he started to fall.

He was still falling when the Colt blasted from

below, two shots only. *Must've only had time to thumb two loads in!* The thought flashed into his head even as he fought to stay on his feet, hearing the bullets whistle past.

He grabbed wildly at the crumbling edge and tried to pull himself forward. He managed it a little, then the edge caught him across the chest, driving the breath from him as he tumbled down the steep slope.

He rolled and skidded, and when he sprawled on the narrow trail he almost passed out with the jarring that drove out whatever little breath remained in his lungs. His legs hung over the edge and he flailed wildly, rolling his body on to more solid ground, swinging his legs in last.

He yelled as something seared his left calf and kicked that leg into a painful angle. But he kept his body rolled up and skidded around the bend, grabbing wildly at some rocks, pulling himself in behind them.

Over the next minute or two there were several more shots; the last two came close to nailing him, striking the rocks and ricocheting, stinging one side of his face with gravel. The skin broke and the blood flowed.

He lay there, gasping, and spotted his rifle a few feet away. It lay on the ground and the barrel seemed to be clear of loose dirt that might block it; he was pretty certain it hadn't dug in and, without intending to, he hurled himself down the slope and rolled and slid almost on top of the weapon, reaching for it.

He pulled it against his body, his groping hands

already working the lever, swinging the barrel to the front. The other man was on the edge of the trail up there now, squinting in the sunlight. His face was in full view of Clint Reid, a hard, unshaven face, with a large nose and a slash for a mouth and eyes that could have doubled as gun muzzles.

'Whoever you are, mister,' a deep voice called down to him, 'you ain't got long to live.'

'Maybe it's *you* that ain't got long,' shouted Clint whipping the rifle to his shoulder and firing two fast shots.

He saw gravel spurt behind the killer on the rocky wall, and the bullets snarled, The man dropped to one knee and fired three fast shots with the Colt. Clint grinned tightly.

That would have been his complete load! Now the killer had an empty gun again. . . .

Clint got off two more shots before the other dodged around the bend, surprised to hear a horse whinnying and, soon after, the clatter of hoofs – dwindling fast.

He stayed put, rifle cocked, eyes restless, ears straining to hear if the hoofbeats were coming in his direction – but there was nothing now: even the birdlife that had been disturbed by the gunfire seemed to be settling down again.

'Well, next thing I better do,' he told himself quietly, 'is go take a look at the feller who got shot.'

He already knew the man was dead, but figured it was the right thing to do. *Right thing?* He moaned slightly.

Yeah! He would have to tell the law about what he'd seen, too. And he was a man who preferred to have as little as possible to do with the law.

He hoped the killer was still riding away from here – fast!

The Laramie sheriff was Si McLaren, a man in his sixties, experienced, unsmiling, and showing his age. He had a stub of a cheroot between his teeth, damp from his saliva, and now he leaned over to his left and spat. The cheroot stub made a dull clang when it hit the side of the battered old grease can that was being used as a wastebin.

He had a craggy face, bristly with a two- or three-day growth of beard, and he scratched this stubble as he stared up at Clint Reid from his creaky swivel-chair.

'Reid, huh?' He glanced at the paper before him, read aloud: 'Clinton Adamson Reid. Family name, that? *Adamson?*'

'My mother's maiden name. You been doing some checking?'

'You'd be the one mangled Slip Riley's hand,' said McLaren, ignoring Reid's query. It wasn't a question and Reid merely nodded.

'They tell me you changed your grip on that six-gun so fast there's still argument about whether you took it out butt first from your holster, all ready to club somethin', an' did just that.' There was a question in his voice.

'I drew, ready to shoot, but didn't see the need, so

23

changed my grip, and clubbed his hand instead.'

'Mighty sure of yourself – but Riley's been a pain for a long time. Still, a man who did to him what you did. . . .' The lawman shook his head slowly. 'Well, it was mighty brutal.'

Clint decided that that didn't need a comment.

'I'm trying to tell you about the man I saw killed, in the hills, Sheriff. Cold-blooded murder.'

The sheriff held his gaze steady for a long minute, then gave a jerky nod. 'Yeah, sure sounds like it. An' you seen the feller who done it?' At Clint's affirmative nod, the lawman continued: 'He took a shot at you, you say?'

'Several. Said I only had a short time to live.'

' 'Cause you'd seen him do the killin'. Yeah. Which I would take to mean that he figures you could identify him?'

'I could,' Clint said emphatically.

'Describe him.'

'Big feller, maybe no taller than me, but half as wide again. Had this long brown hair – sort of tousled, but you could see it had a natural curl – or maybe a wave to it. And he had a beak an eagle would kill for.'

The sheriff gave a half-smile. 'And. . . ?'

'That's about it, I guess. He crouched pretty quick and put those three shots into the feller that'd been runnin' away. Oh, I *think*, but I ain't sure, he could've had a joint missing from his trigger finger.'

The lawman just nodded, not showing any surprise. 'Yeah, the missing finger-joint nails him all right. Rawley Forbes. Mean son of a bitch, but mostly after he's been hittin' the booze. Makes moonshine in a still I ain't yet found back in them hills. There's a coupla things I'd like to nail him on, but, goddammit, he always seems to slip by.'

'Well, glad you recognize him, Sheriff. You get a posse together nice and fast and you'll likely be able to tie him up in those hills.'

'Knows 'em like the back of his hand. He'd lead us one helluva chase. But he comes to town every so often to pick up stores and stuff to make his booze.'

Clint Reid frowned. 'You're gonna wait till he comes to *you*?'

'Be the easiest way. Too bad you didn't think to bring in the dead feller.'

'Judas, Sheriff! Forbes or whoever he is had already told me he'd be after me, so I came in quick as I could to tell you what happened.'

'Yeah, 'preciate that. But I still need to get Rawley's side of the story.'

'Hell! *His* side of it is that he killed a man. Deliberate murder! And I saw him – and he *knows* I did. Why, he threatened me. . . .'

'Now, he didn't *actually* do that, did he?'

'What? Telling me I didn't have long to live, then shooting at me? By hell! I see that as good as a threat as you'll get.'

The sheriff stared up at him, sighed, then took a pipe from his shirt pocket, placed the stem between his teeth, and reached for a pouch on his desk. He proceeded to stuff tobacco into the pipe bowl and spoke without looking up, concentrating on the filling of the bowl.

'You tangled with the law at all, son?'

Clint tensed. Those cold eyes were penetrating.

'I don't have any kinda record. You won't find my name on any Wanted dodgers.'

'Sounds like you're dodgin' the issue, son.'

Clint sighed. 'I'm not! All right, there was a shoot-out in Trinidad, Colorado, couple, three years ago. I was with a trail herd, young and full of vinegar, and we all got likkered-up and started eyein'-off the gals and – well, the local fellers didn't like it. Got mightily outta hand and the saloon got wrecked, half the town was shot up badly: bunch of the townsmen agin a bunch of us trailmen. No one died but there was a few wounded on both sides and a lot of damage done.' He paused, shrugged. 'Me, with my luck, I was the one wounded the sheriff's son. He had me beat up, kicked outta town, and spread the word I was a heller an'—'

'Thought I recognized the name. Got it on a list some lawman from down south sent up. You got guts. still usin' your own name, I'll say that. That sher'ff sure don't like you.'

'The kid was half-drunk and drew first. Someone tossed an empty bottle and it hit my gun arm, threw off my aim. I nailed him in the hip and he don't walk so good now.' He let the rest trail off and the silence dragged. Finally Clint added, 'That's why I like it up here in the north. That sheriff has a long memory and I damn near starved trying to find work after he spread the word I was a killer and so on.'

'Well, that's your side of the story,' the sheriff observed, and held up a hand quickly as Clint's face tightened. 'Relax, son. I was testin' you. You told the truth and that makes you OK in my book. But I'll need your stuff about Rawley Forbes in writin' and then we'll go see who the hell it was he shot.'

'Wondered when someone was gonna get around to wonderin' who the dead man is. Not that you'll find any identification on him. Forbes went through his pockets so I wouldn't reckon you'd even find a pinch of fluff in 'em.'

The lawman heaved to his feet with a series of grunts, stretched his arms a little, then winced and grabbed his left shoulder.

'Blamed rheumatism! All right, Mr Clinton Adamson Reid, you write me your statement and then we'll go take a look.'

'Forbes'll be long gone by then.'

'Son, I know Rawley; he could already be gone – claim he's been nowhere near that place for days or longer. But we still gotta go take a look, so let's hustle.'

CHAPTER 3

ALIBI

It took longer to reach Rawley Forbes's spread going by the regular trail than it had when Clint Reid had cut across country following the wandering tracks of his heifer.

It was larger than Clint's place, probably about double the size and the cabin a good deal more substantial, a real ranch house.

Clint figured Forbes's cattle would nearly triple the number he was at present running. Forbes had the grass and water to handle it, too.

There were two riders hazing-in a bunch of steers to a fresh pasture when Si McLaren and Clint Reid rode in. They slowed going up the slope to where the riders were and Clint said:

'That big rider – looks about the same size as Forbes, but he's wearing different clothes, even the hat.'

'Uh-huh,' grunted the sheriff, looking tired from the long ride out.

Clint frowned. 'You know the other man?'

'Yeah. Hank Purcell. Hardcase, works the ranches a couple days here, couple there. They say he used to be a barber, believe it or not. Then decided he wanted to be a real dyed-in-the-wool cowboy.'

'You got a . . . funny tone when you say that. Something special about him?'

'Not that I know of. Suspect he's hidin' from somethin' in his past but . . . just a hunch, nothin' definite. Real tough, and he's been in a few bloody brawls – rough ones . . . and he's mighty friendly with Forbes.'

Reid's frown deepened as the lawman kept looking at him. 'Hell! You reckon Purcell's gonna give Forbes an alibi?'

'I do. An' I'll take bettin' money if you figure I'm wrong.'

Clint's jaws hardened. 'Look, Sheriff, I told you what I saw and it's gospel. If Forbes has fixed himself an alibi and says I *didn't* see him kill that other feller, then he's a liar.'

'I wouldn't call him that to his face, son.'

'If I'm calling him that at all, it *will* be to his face.'

The lawman nodded gently. 'Right respectful thinkin', son. But let's see what develops.' He narrowed his eyes a little, adding: 'I've waited a long time to really nail his hide to the wall. And this time I might just do it.'

But it was hard for Clint's story to sound like it was

29

the truth. To start with, Rawley Forbes was wearing different clothes, still ranch work-clothes, but a brown shirt instead of the blue one Clint had seen him in, a faded, battered grey hat, with a peak and a long groove holding it that way, whereas the hat Clint had seen was a dirty, fawn, flat-crowned Stetson. The trousers were striped now and twin Colts were on his hips. He lifted his hat briefly to wipe sweat from his forehead with a spotted kerchief and Clint stiffened when he saw neatly trimmed, curly hair, flattened a little by the hat and some sort of hair grease that made it gleam.

'Christ!' Clint murmured. 'He's had a haircut!' He looked sharply at McLaren. 'You thinking what I am?'

'Might be. I've heard that Hank Purcell makes a little extra cash barberin' some of the cowboys workin' these ranges.'

'Hell!' The word exploded from Reid, sure now that Forbes was going to have an alibi all arranged – neat and tidy.

The rancher greeted the sheriff in a friendly manner and gave Clint a brief amiable nod. *Mighty confident.*

Reid had a sick feeling developing in his belly.

'Howdy, Si. Not often we see you out this way. Can you wait'll Hank an' me haze this bunch into the brandin' pen? Then we'll brew a cup of coffee an' yarn. OK?'

'Coffee sounds good, Rawley, but somethin' I gotta ask you right now.'

30

Forbes looked interested, but let his annoyance show as he sent Purcell to sort out the herd, which was jostling to get through the chute to the pen now.

'Just open the gate an' push 'em through, Hank.' Then he turned back to the sheriff. 'Well, Si?'

'We had a report that you shot a man up here in the hills.'

Forbes lifted in his stirrups, glanced briefly at Clint. 'Shot someone? Judas Priest! Who said that? Who am I s'posed to've shot?' He gave a brief grin and looked at Hank Purcell as the man came riding back from the branding pen. 'An' I wonder when I done it! Hey, Hank – how long we been roundin'-up and hazin' these critters?'

'Since before full daylight, boss.' Hank glanced at the sheriff. 'Hell, Si, I'm all stiff an' creaky, we done so much ridin' to get these beeves together. Was just dreamin' of coffee an' grub when you rode up with this – eyewash about Rawley shootin' someone.'

'*Eyewash*, you reckon?' said the lawman tersely. 'What you gotta say about that, son?'

Clint looked squarely at Forbes. 'A few hours ago I saw you shoot a man three times – in cold blood. Right up there above that zigzag trail. Can't quite see it from here but when you saw me, an' knew I must've seen you do it, you told me I wouldn't be living long.'

'And you damn well won't, you keep tellin' lies like that about me.' Rawley Forbes was angry and dropped one hand to the butt of a six-gun.

'Quit that, Rawl!' snapped McLaren, his own Colt

31

coming up at surprising speed.

Forbes frowned, then lifted his hand away from the gun. 'Look, Si, you ain't been listening to this . . . drifter or whoever he is, have you? I've never seen him before, but I got a notion he's the one workin' a spread on Buckshot Ridge, right?' By way of reply, all he got was a curt nod from Reid. Then he turned back to the sheriff. 'What the hell you think I am, Si?'

'Not sure, Rawl, but I do know you got a hot temper and if you cared to notch your guns, you'd have mighty rough butts to grip.'

'Aw, come on, Si. I know I've kicked over the traces now and again, but, hell! Who hasn't? I mean, you work your butt off from bare daylight till after dark every day of your damn life. You fight them cunnin' cows and they get into some of the god*damnedest* places where you gotta go to haze 'em out. Full of snakes or wolves. An' . . . well, you know what I mean! Man builds up a lotta tension and has to bust loose every so often. I always pay for any damages.'

'Wreckin' a saloon or kickin' in the door of a whorehouse ain't what I'm talkin' about, Rawley. This is a man's life.'

'*Who*? Who the hell'm I s'posed to've shot?'

'Hell! Rawl ain't no killer,' said Hank vehemently.

'Now, that could be debatable, Hank, but. . . .' McLaren swung his gaze back to the rancher and there was reluctant doubt creeping into his tone and looks. 'I dunno who you're s'posed to've killed, Rawl, not yet. But young Clint Reid here maintains it was on your south range, just below the ridge. S'pose we ride up and take a look?'

Forbes frowned, glanced at Purcell, who had his lips pursed. 'I – dunno, Si. I mean . . . Hank, you reckon you and the boys can get them steers branded by sundown? We gotta ship 'em to Cheyenne, under contract, Si, an' it means drivin' 'em down to the siding in time to make the train.'

'It'd be mighty close, boss,' cut in Purcell.

'Well, dammit, Si. You can see the bind I'm in. I just gotta sell them steers. I owe the feed-'n-grain store an' couple other places. I *gotta* get 'em to Cheyenne. Money's kinda tight for me right now.'

'Your problem, Rawley,' McLaren told him: no sympathy. Forbes swore loud and long and the lawman turned to Hank. 'Go get one of your crew to help you.'

'Means takin' someone away from a job he's already doin',' protested Forbes and then he saw the stubborn look on the old lawman's face. He spat and threw up his hands. 'OK, OK! Hank, do what you can.' He glared at Clint Reid. 'And just who the hell *are* you, anyway, feller?'

'I'm Clint Reid, the one saw you kill a man up there on the high trail. You took a couple of shots at me as well.'

Forbes looked at Hank, stunned, then shrugged and shouted: 'By hell! Mr Clint Reid – you – are – a goddamn – *liar*!'

'Now hold up!' shouted Sheriff McLaren quickly.

But his words went unheeded.

Clint Reid suddenly threw himself bodily from the

saddle, crashed into Rawley Forbes, and the pair of them tumbled to the ground with a thud and gusting breaths. Immediately they started fighting, punching awkwardly in their tangled positions, dust and dirt flying, causing the mounts to whinny and back up.

'*Cut it out*!' bawled McLaren, but his words were drowned out for the fighters by their own grunting and rolling about on the ground, until Reid took a blow on the side of his head that sent him sliding down the slope. Forbes, blood streaming from his nostrils, leapt after him, teeth bared, ready to continue combat.

McLaren started to draw his gun but when it was halfway out of leather he suddenly rammed it back in, folded his hands on the saddle horn after backing his horse up a few paces so he could get a better view of the continuing brawl.

'You stay put, Hank,' he said, and Purcell reluctantly settled back in his saddle and watched the fight.

They were much of a match in size, though Forbes had the advantage of heavier shoulders and upper body in general.

When he landed a punch Reid knew it, staggering back several feet in his struggle to maintain balance, and, at the same time, dodge the barrage of blows Forbes was following through with. He tasted blood. His mouth went numb when hard knuckles crushed his lips against his teeth, none of which – luckily – broke.

But, by *God*! it was damned painful and this pain

surged through Clint and drove him wild. He stepped back in to meet Forbes's follow-through, slammed the punch aimed at his eyes aside with his left forearm and planted his right fist in the middle of Forbes's face.

The man stopped as if hauled back by a rope around his neck, head snapping back, blood flying from his mangled nose, legs dancing frantically, as he fought for balance. Clint Reid kept coming at him, thrusting forward, first a right, then a left following so closely it was a wonder the fists didn't tangle. Forbes, the bulkier man, tottered and took a wild step sideways so as to keep balance, but suddenly Reid was there, hammering his ribs, his jaw, and dammit! – his ear. Man! Now that hurt!

Rawley Forbes let out a yell and, trying to see through tears squeezed from his eyes by the surge of pain, suddenly held his ground. It caught Clint by surprise and he walked smack into a barrage of blows that had him retreating until his feet tangled and he went down – not quite all the way: his left hand spread out on the ground and stopped him from falling any further.

Forbes closed for the kill, swung a boot at Reid's supporting arm and kicked it away. Clint fell on his side but rolled in towards Forbes, who, not expecting this, stumbled over his body and began to fall. Clint rolled aside so the man didn't land on top of him, grunted as he twisted and got some leverage from his bent legs.

The top of his head rammed into Forbes's upper

chest and the onlookers heard the clack of Forbes's teeth. His head went back and his body followed, aided by a swinging boot from Clint Reid. It landed squarely on the rancher's left side, sent him skidding away to fall on his face.

He lay there, panting, groaning, and, arms feeling as heavy as assault cannons, Reid moved in with slow steps.

A gunshot stopped him and he snapped his head around to see Sheriff McLaren holding his smoking six-gun.

'Reckon that's enough, boys. You keep on, someone's gonna get hurt.'

'*Gonna* get hurt?' gasped Clint. 'If this ain't – hurt – then I – I don't wanna find out – what – is. How about you, feller?'

Rawley Forbes swayed as he blinked and wiped blood coming from a gash on his forehead out of his eyes. Even through the swelling and smeared blood, Reid saw the hate in those eyes. But Forbes nodded, held up a hand with skinned knuckles.

'C-call it . . . quits,' he muttered hoarsely. 'I – can't afford – to be – banged up with – all the work I gotta – do around here.'

McLaren looked from one to the other. 'Waste of time askin' you to shake hands, I s'pose.' Both men's shoulders stiffened at the suggestion and they shook their heads.

'Well, best wash up at yonder creek. Then we go look at this place where you're s'posed to've shot someone, Rawley.'

36

' "S'posed to" – is – right,' slurred Forbes, glaring at Clint as he sluiced cold, murky water over his head and face.

'*Leave it!*' snapped the sheriff, hand on gun butt, as both men looked as if they might start fighting again. 'Man who throws the next punch gets to see my cells from the inside – an' I tell you true, they ain't been cleaned out for a week, Been full of drunks, so you know what you'll find. Just wash up a mite more and we'll get under way.'

They couldn't find the exact place where Clint swore he had seen Rawley Forbes shoot the unknown man.

Forbes looked at him in exasperation. 'Listen, feller, you've made this damn accusation and this is where you claim the murder happened. You can describe it again and we'll find every damn landmark necessary to arrive – right – here. And I don't see no dead bodies.'

Clint returned the hostile gaze levelly. 'That part of the trail wasn't collapsed when I saw you shoot that ranny.' He pointed to where a section of the winding trail had slid away down the slope and ended in a pile of rubble and rocks and clods of earth some ten feet below.

Forbes just shook his head slowly, looking disgusted. 'Christ, man, I rode along here – must be a week ago now – and it was one continuous trail. Now it's collapsed, and, dammit-to-hell, that's just what this country does! Judas, Si, you know how unstable it is in parts. That's why we hardly ever use these trails.'

37

'So, what were you doin' up here a week ago?' McLaren asked mildly.

'Chasin' one of my best stud bulls! Randy sonuver went after couple my cows and they ran into this neck of the woods. Hell, I wouldn't come up here unless I had to.' Forbes looked coldly at Clint. 'And I *had* to; had to get my cows down safely to the other pastures. Was no signs of it givin' way then but we did have that half-day of rain, three, four days back, Si. Coulda loosened things up.'

McLaren nodded. 'He's right, Clint. Coulda loosened the ground an' it finally carried away under its own weight. Happens around these parts, time to time.'

'I savvy that's possible, but there hadn't been any landslip a few hours back. And this looks recent. See the colour of the soil? Kinda dark, whereas some of that other soil on the slope that hasn't . . . moved . . . is pale and powdery-lookin' from bein' long exposed to the sun.'

'Goddammit, Si! This *hombre*, for whatever reason, is out to get me. He's findin' all kindsa things to back up his stupid story.'

'Hmmm. Is kinda pushin' things,' admitted the sheriff. 'You ever know Rawley before, mebbe, son? Got an old score to settle, or that kinda thing?'

'No! I *ain't* got any score to settle. I seen him shoot some ranny three times right where we're standin' – or mebbe a few feet along where it's dropped away now. I *saw* it happen and he spotted me before I could get away, took a few shots at me and told me I din' have long to live.'

'That last part's true,' Forbes admitted. 'I been missin' a couple steers up this way and I figured he might've been helpin' himself to some free beef. I was just – warnin' him off, Si.'

'So you have seen him before. You're changin' your story, Rawley,' the lawman said quietly. 'You said before you hadn't been up here recently.'

Forbes shrugged. 'Well, I bin kinda wonderin' – this feller claimin' he saw me kill some unknown ranny – if mebbe *he* hasn't killed someone up here and seen a chance to put the blame on me, as it's my land.'

'Now why the hell would I do that?' Clint demanded. 'Till I saw you run outta the trees, I never even knew you existed. And I'm damn well wishing right now that you didn't!'

'You wanna do somethin' about that?' Forbes dropped a hand towards his holstered gun but the sheriff waved his own Colt and the rancher just lifted his hands out to the sides. 'OK, Si. I'll try to relax. But you tell this sonuver to keep his mouth off me or—'

'Mebbe I'll shut both your mouths!' the lawman snapped, obviously irritated, if not downright angry by now. 'Look you, Reid, you've made accusations and, puttin' most of 'em aside for now – we still ain't seen any dead man!'

'Yeah!' said Forbes quickly. 'Where the hell *is* this man I'm s'posed to've shot?'

Clint had been wondering that himself; he

39

pointed down to where the trail had collapsed. 'At a guess I'd say under a couple of tons of that dirt down there. Kinda . . . lucky, it collapsin' like that.'

McLaren craned his neck exaggeratedly as he looked over the broken edge. 'You wanta start diggin', son? Reckon Rawley here could find you a shovel to borrow. . . .'

Clint was agitated now. His mind was spinning.

What could've happened? and *How did it happen?'* and *Why had it happened?*

'You look kinda flimflammed, son. You feel the need to change *your* story, mebbe. . . ?'

'*No*! Goddammit, I don't!'

'Well, *I* want some kinda apology,' snapped Forbes, glaring, right hand twitching a little closer to his gun butt.

'Forget it, Rawley,' grated the lawman, his own gun half-drawn. 'This is all kinda – sideways – somehow. 'Cain't think of why this feller would ride in and make these claims, seein' as he's a total stranger to us all. He admits he don't know you so he ain't tryin' to put you down because of some grudge or the like. You say you weren't here when he said, nor you done what he said. There ain't no body. . . .' He glanced down to the heap of rubble below. 'Unless someone wants to get some exercise. . . . No? Well, I guess I can savvy that. So here's what I propose. . . .' He looked from one man to the other, let them sweat a little, then said, 'We forget the whole blame thing.'

Forbes smiled and nodded. 'I'm with you, Si. I got nothin' agin this feller. Mebbe he was drunk, slept

40

rough, even, and had nightmares an' come up with this—'

'Let's not get too carried away, Rawl,' broke in the sheriff. 'Reid? You got anything to say?'

'No. If I say what I'd like to, you'd throw me in that lousy jail cell and have me cleanin' it up. So, I say to hell with it, too.' They were all nodding, as this seemed to be the simplest solution. Then Clint added: 'For now. You want a murderer walkin' around your bailiwick, that's your business, McLaren.'

The sheriff narrowed his old rheumy eyes and Forbes tensed, giving Reid a murderous glare.

'*For now. . . ?* The hell's that mean?'

'Means I'll leave things as they are. Right now I want to get back to my own spread. But I'll be around for a while, give it a little more thought, mebbe come back to look around.'

'You come on to my land and I'll damn well shoot you for trespassin'!' snapped Forbes, looking like he meant it.

'Watch what you say, Rawley,' warned the sheriff quietly. 'Both of you just go about your business. If – and I say *if* I think this needs further lookin' into, then I'll do it. You both savvy that? 'Cause if there's any doubt – I still need that jail cell washed out so it's fit for human habitation. My advice to you boys is to think that over.'

'Might be a good idea, Rawl,' cut in Hank Purcell. 'There's somethin' – loco here. Gotta be some reason why this Reid feller come up with his story.'

'*These lies*, you mean,' snapped the still angry Forbes.

'That's it!' said McLaren. 'Leave it – right there.'

His gun was still in his hand and he moved it so it was between Reid and Forbes, easy to swing either way.

'Fine with me!' growled Forbes. 'I got nothin' to hide, but by Godfrey, I got one helluva round-up to finish and then the trail drive to Cheyenne if I don't wanna miss that train.' He set his hard gaze on Clint Reid. 'I'll get around to you later.'

'Any time.'

'No!' barked the sheriff. 'It stays just as it is. *I*'ll do any more checkin'. And I'm goin' on record to say that either of you two get in my way, you're both lookin' at jail time . . .' he paused, let a brief silence drag, then, 'or lookin' down the barrel of my gun. Savvy?'

Both Reid and Forbes nodded curtly; they both knew McLaren's reputation, and his rheumatics hadn't slowed him down much with a gun yet.

But Rawley Forbes had the last word, standing frowning at Clint Reid.

'Sure as hell would like to know why you come outta nowhere and try to pin a killin' on me, feller. Surely would.'

'Just stick around – you'll find out.'

Riding away eventually, Clint noticed how grumpy and surly the sheriff was. 'You kinda – backed off in a hurry.'

'Was goin' nowhere. You said he done it, he said he didn't. It don't mean I'm lettin' it slide.'

'You could still get him on my evidence, couldn't you, Sheriff?'

McLaren glanced across as they rode along the bank of a creek. 'I'd like to be damn sure. I've been tryin' since Moses was a pup – or so it seems – to get Rawley for *somethin'*. Every damn time, he ducks out. Thought we mighta had him now, but all that barberin' and change of clothes and Hank backin' him up – well, sort of makes it – a leetle bit – vague.'

'I won't be changing my story,' Clint said flatly.

'Wasn't askin' you to!' snapped the lawman. 'Ah – I'm just edgy about the deal, is all. We might manage to nail him yet. Leastways, I sure as hell hope so! He's gettin' cockier by the day. Time I made him pull his horns in.'

'Thought we had him cold-decked, but he's collapsed that damn trail now and the body's buried under all that rubble.'

'No body, no charge,' the lawman said bitterly.

'What're you looking at me like that for?' Clint suddenly demanded.

'Just sizin' you up.'

'Hell!'

Forbes and Purcell looked down on the lawman and Clint as they rode away.

'Think they'll ever start diggin', Rawl?' Hank asked.

'Doubt it.' The rancher looked suddenly grim. 'I oughta make *you* start, using that full stick of dynamite. Damn well told you a half would do.'

Hank looked back steadily. 'I know. Just wanted to make sure, was all.'

'You did that! Buried five boxes of guns, as well. Now I'm out five thousand dollars, and if we don't get this trail drive under way we're gonna be eatin' hardtack and jerky for a month – if the Injuns don't scalp us when they don't get those guns. I can't come up with the money to buy more.'

Hank looked contrite and a little hurt.

It was important to him that Forbes thought well of him – always.

CHAPTER 4

'MY MISTAKE!'

The sheriff detained Clint longer than the rancher would have liked when they got back to town.

'It's all there in my statement, Sheriff,' Clint said edgily, pointing to the several sheets of paper covered in his writing. 'Look, I want to see Belle before I go back to my spread. You keep me here much longer and I won't get away before dark, dammit!'

Si McLaren looked up slowly and then his lips moved in a flash of a smile. 'Just givin' you time to cool off, son. You and Forbes're both a couple hot-heads and I don't want another shootin' on my hands. I'm workin' too hard as it is now you've brought me this story.'

'Hell, Sheriff! It's true! Forbes had set things up to make it look like a lot of eyewash, but I did see what I've written down here. He did the shooting.

Now he's collapsed that trail with half a stick of dynamite or something, and Hank Purcell has barbered him so his hair ain't flying all around his head like it was when I saw him. But what I told you is still true. He was the one who murdered that man in cold blood.'

'Would be a help if we knew just who this dead feller was – or if there is a dead feller at all.'

On the other side of the desk Clint reared back, his face hardening. 'I – dunno as I could get my gun out faster'n you, McLaren, but you're close to calling me a liar.'

The lawman held up a hand wearily. 'I'm only saying it would make everythin' a whole damn sight easier if we had a body. We're never gonna break Forbes's alibi.'

'Unless you dig the body out from under that collapsed trail. And with all that dirt on top of him you'd be lucky to find somethin' you could even identify as what might've been a human body, let alone the three slugs that killed him.'

'Yeah, well, you see, that's the problem, ain't it? Rawley Forbes knows we ain't gonna do that; not enough funds for one thing – and not on the word of a stranger we know nothin' about.'

Clint started to bristle at that but made himself calm down. 'Sheriff, I'm tired of saying it, but *I saw what I said I saw!* Now it's gonna be hard as hell to prove, but way I see it, that's your problem, I've done my part. It's your business from here on in.'

'Aw, now wait up, son. I know it's kinda mixed up,

and I have to tell you, I'm inclined to take your word as gospel. . . .'

'Big of you!'

'Keep your shirt on. Look at it from my angle.'

'I know. You're getting old and you don't want anything too complicated, and you don't have the funds and so on. I savvy all that. But now I seem to be caught up in something I'd rather do without. Hell! I only wanted to do the right thing. And all I want now is to get my ranch fixed up so Belle and I can get married and move in.'

McLaren eased back in his chair, those old eyes probing deeply into Clint Reid – or so he felt. 'Your bad luck, seein' what you did, son, but you did do the right thing. Look, I believe you or we wouldn't be sittin' here right now, but there's nothin' more I can do. Forbes has outsmarted us both: he's got an alibi and knows how to act innocent, and Hank Purcell will back him all the way. And – we – ain't – got – a – damn – body!'

'You're saying he's gonna get away with' it?'

'The hell he is!' McLaren snorted. 'Rawley Forbes thinks he's a law unto himself. He's buffaloed a lot of folk so he's gotten away with a lot of things he shouldn't've. Aw, mebbe I'm to blame here and there. Old age slows me down and I don't have the get-up-an'-go I once had. But, if I had a young deputy with a conscience—'

'Stop right there! I got no ambitions to be any kind of a lawman. I'm a cowboy and I aim to stay that way. All I want to do is work up a paying ranch, with a good wife at my side and a couple of kids later on. That's my life as I see it. Period!'

The sheriff sighed. 'Well, I know Belle Camden and she's a fine woman. You're the first to get her to agree to marriage. I ain't gonna try to bust that up; but, son, I won't press you, but I am disappointed – mighty disappointed. I respect your integrity, wish you luck with your ranch and Belle – or mebbe I shoulda said that the other way round. In any case, I'd like to know that you'll be on hand if I get myself in a real bind – somethin' I just can't handle without help.'

'Hell! You'll have me cryin' along with you in a minute,' broke in Reid. He sighed heavily. 'I guess I can give you my word that if you *really* can't handle things then I'll . . . I'll see if I can lend a hand. But I'll be the judge of that. That all right?'

McLaren smiled and there was a mischievous satisfaction in the old eyes and in the twitch of his mouth.

'Son, I guess I'm just gonna *have* to be satisfied with that.'

'You are. *Now*, can I go see Belle?'

The lawman waved casually towards the office door.

'I ain't stoppin' you.'

As he passed the desk on his way out Clint murmured, 'You cunning old son of a – *gun*!'

He was sure he heard the lawman chuckle as he closed the door behind him.

*

'Well, where is she? I told her I'd pick her up here this afternoon, and I got delayed by that cunning old lawman – and now it's almost dusk.'

Mitch Camden was Belle's elder brother, a gaunt man who enjoyed bookwork, especially when it was associated with his growing ranch, the Rocking C, where Belle stayed with him and his family. He looked at Reid now and saw his rising agitation.

'Well, Clint, I don't know what arrangements you'd originally made with Belle, but she got a message you wanted to meet her at that little lake on your land and have a . . . "starlight supper" I believe is what she said . . . barbecue or something. She went off with a packed picnic basket.'

'When the hell was this? I never sent her any damn message.'

'Why, that kid who runs errands for just about anyone in town: "Legs" someone or other. He brought it.'

'Legs Jenner – but who asked him to give Belle the message?'

'I don't know. I thought it must've been you.'

'Goddammit to hell!'

'I know the kid said he was given a quarter . . . and. . . . Well! *Adios* to you, too, future brother-in-law.' Mitch Camden sounded peeved as he called after Reid, who had turned abruptly and stomped out of the ranch house.

Legs Jenner was waiting for him when he got back to town and tentatively held out a folded piece of paper.

49

'For you, Mr Reid. He said you'd likely gimme a quarter for bringin' it to you.'

A little breathless, Clint skidded his horse to a stop. He looked at the dirty, freckled face of the boy in his patched clothes as he took the proffered note.

'I'll give you a quarter if you tell me who gave you this.'

One grubby hand pointed in the air as Clint showed the boy a shiny quarter between his thumb and finger.

'Was Mr Purcell. He works for—'

'Yeah, I know who he works for, boy. Here: don't make yourself sick on sticky candy bars.'

The kid ran off, yodelling in his happiness, and Clint slowly unfolded the sheet of paper. There were just a few words printed on it in ink:

YOU MADE A MISTAKE. WE THINK YOU OUGHT TO TELL MCLAREN. THE GAL DOES TOO.

There was no signature, of course, and his hands shook as he read the words: *The gal does too.*

To him, that meant only one thing: that they had hold of her – whoever 'they' were.

'Goddamn you, Forbes!' he said aloud and a couple of passers-by veered a yard or two away from where he stood looking murderous. 'Maybe *I*'m not the one who made the mistake. It could be *you*, and the biggest mistake you ever make will be if you harm Belle in any way – *any way.*'

He crumpled the note into his shirt pocket, then turned his mount and rode back towards the law office.

Sheriff McLaren had seen him coming through his grimy office window and was able to read his body language correctly as he opened the door and Clint came striding up, face grim.

'Trouble, son?'

'Er . . . well, I been wonderin', Sheriff. Feller I saw do the shootin' was all ragged and had long, dirty-looking hair flying around his face. Can't stop thinking about how neat and clean this Rawley Forbes was when we saw him. Just – don't seem like it could be the same man.'

McLaren stiffened and stared long and hard at Clint Reid. He said, quietly, 'I didn't know better, son, I might think you was tryin to tell me that – now – for some reason – you ain't sure it was Forbes you saw.'

Reid looked mighty uncomfortable, slid his gaze away from contact with the lawman's. 'It's been nagging at me. Starting to worry me that if I *did* make a mistake – well – Forbes ain't what you call a likeable man, fact I think he's scum, but those things don't matter when it's a genuine mistake, do they? What matters is, whoever made it has to set it right, soon as he can.'

'Ye-ah. That'd be the right and fair thing to do, all right. Is that what you're tellin' me? I mean – I want to hear you *say* it, if you genu-ine-ly think – *feel* – you've made a mistake accusin' Rawley Forbes.'

Clint did everything but squirm. He couldn't hold McLaren's hard, cold, expectant gaze.

'I'm waitin', son.'

'Been thinkin' hard about it, Sheriff.'

'Can see that. You're right upset. Tell me what seems to be the trouble.'

'I – I think . . . mebbe I did make a mistake. More I turn it over in my mind, the more I—'

'Just what kind of mistake?' McLaren asked flatly, offering no help beyond those few words. 'Spell it out, boy. This is your story.'

Clint licked his lips and his swallowing was clearly audible. 'I just can't see the Forbes we met as that long-haired crazy son of a bitch, who ran outta the trees and stood over that feller and – pumped three shots into him, cold as you like. 'Specially that last shot. It just wasn't necessary: the others had already finished him. Takes a really cold-blooded man to do that kinda thing.'

'So, what you're sayin' is, you've had a change of mind and it lets Rawley Forbes off the *goddamn hook*?'

Clint winced as the sheriff shouted the last two words, but then his jaw firmed and he gave a jerky nod.

'That's it, McLaren. I – I'm mighty sorry but—'

'How'd they get to you?' McLaren cut in harshly. 'No! Don't look like that – and don't lie to me no more.'

'Hey! Just a goddamn minute. You can't—'

'Aw, shut *up*, Reid! Don't climb on your high hoss with me. You've turned yaller, been frightened off by how powerful Forbes is, turned your guts – if you have any – to water.'

'I don't have to stand here and listen to this. Hell, I don't like Forbes any better'n you do, but I – I won't railroad an innocent man or one who *might* be innocent – just so you can close your damn books and go fishing.'

'You goin'? Or you want me to throw you out? An' don't think I can't do it, age an' rheumatics an' all.'

Reid's teeth tugged at his bottom lip, then he squared his shoulders and walked towards the door.

'I'm sorry, McLaren. I really am. But it's just somethin' I have to do. Matter of conscience.'

'Matter of somethin'. Not conscience. More likely *backbone* – or the lack of it. Now git. An' make that right outta my town. I don't want to see you or hear of you in it one hour from now.'

Teeth clamped, fists clenched, Clint Reid went out and closed the door quietly behind him.

The sheriff kicked his desk chair violently and hurt his foot before spinning around and dropping into it, teeth gritted.

The bastards! How in hell'd they get to that boy!

Then he remembered Belle and he was sorry for the way he had bad-mouthed Clint Reid.

'Aw, son,' he muttered, 'I think I savvy now. Goddammittohell! The one and only way they could get to you, and Forbes found it.'

CHAPTER 5

RETURN

It was full dark by the time Clint Reid saw the lights of the ranch house on the lower slopes of the range that speared through Rawley Forbes's land.

There was a small bunkhouse some distance from the main building and he skirted it carefully on his way to the house. A man stepped out of the shadows, holding a rifle or shotgun – Clint couldn't be sure in the dim light.

'Call out, mister!'

'Clint Reid. I'm here to collect Belle Camden.'

'Belle. . . ? No womenfolk here, mister. Someone's give you a wrong steer.'

Clint stiffened but the way the guard was now holding his gun told him he'd better keep his hands in full view. He folded them on the saddle horn.

'I heard different.'

'Then you oughta get your hearin' checked. . . .'

54

The guard broke off as the ranch-house door opened and a slab of yellow light sliced a few feet into the yard, a man's shadow looming.

'It's all right, Mel. The gal he wants is here. You were out on the range and missed the excitement when Lonnie brought her in after she'd fallen off her horse.'

Clint was already dismounting. 'By God! If she's hurt, Forbes. . . .'

'Judas! You are on a hair-trigger, ain't you, Reid No, she ain't hurt. Bit shaken and maybe got a gravel scar or two, but my cook's seen to her and she's fine. Wanted to take her back to her brother's ranch but she was kinda . . . sure you'd come here lookin' for her.'

'Someone was. Well, I'm here.'

'And you ain't welcome – now or any other time.'

'I'll get outta your hair soon as you send Belle out.'

Forbes – with a crooked smile, Reid thought, but couldn't be sure with the light behind the man's head – called over his shoulder. 'You wanna come see your boyfriend, Belle?'

'Oh, yes!'

Clint felt a surge of relief as soon as he heard her voice and her enthusiasm, then she was standing just outside the door beside Forbes. She smiled at Clint, and proffered a hand to Forbes.

'Thank you for your help, Mr Forbes. I'll be all right now.'

'You're welcome, ma'am – and the name's Rawley. We should be on first names, I reckon, by now.' As

Clint went up the steps to take Belle's arm he saw the leer on the man's face, which, like his own, showed bruises and cuts. Belle quickly clung to Reid's arm with both hands, but before either could speak, Forbes said:

'Got a real gentle little paint all saddled for you, Belle. We'll look after your own hoss till the swellin' in its leg goes down, an' I'll have one of my men deliver it out to the Rockin' C. You are going back there, I take it?'

Belle glanced at Reid, her grip tightening on his arm. 'Eventually, yes. Thank you once again ... Rawley.'

'Pleasure. Reid, she's a right fine lady.'

Clint nodded curtly. 'I agree. My thanks, too, Forbes. For caring for her. *Adios.*'

'Oh! How's old Si? Not too much for him, ridin' all the way out here earlier, was it? I mean, now he knows it was all for nothin' he can relax, I guess. He's a mite old for the job, you ask me.'

'I dunno if he'd agree with that.'

'Oh? Thought he might've give up, seein' as you made a mistake about me, and there's no dead man. S'pose he's not sure where to look now. That is, if he still believes you did see someone shot.'

'Aw, he don't give up that easy. He'll satisfy himself before he does.' Clint paused, watching Forbes's face closely, knowing the man was probing. 'He'll find an answer he likes sometime.'

'Not – around – here.' Forbes's voice was flat but he managed to keep a tight smile showing. 'But *you* come back any time, Belle. You'll be mighty welcome. Just don't bring him.'

She waved, frowning slightly. Then she set the paint alongside Clint's black and they rode away from the ranch.

'You really OK?'

'Of course. Let's go home, Clint.'

He thought she sounded tense.

But they rode sedately away from the ranch and when they had reached the gate and were about to leave Forbes's property, Clint turned and saw that the rancher was still standing in the doorway, watching.

'You're a damn good rider, Belle. You didn't really fall off your horse, did you,' Clint made it a statement rather than a question.

'Why do you doubt me?'

'You know damn well why. I think Forbes or some of his men brought you to his ranch and told you to *say* you had a fall. I'm hoping it's not to help explain away any – injuries?'

She reined up sharply and there was enough starlight for him to see how her grey-green eyes had narrowed and her mouth had tightened.

'Clint, I did fall off my horse. I'm not hurt. I was crossing the river and a couple of Forbes's men were driving a small bunch of cattle along the bank. They put them into the river and my horse got a fright. He scrabbled at the bank and hurt his leg. I rolled over his head and Forbes's men insisted on taking me up to the ranch. I have to say I was treated very well.

'In fact, it was actually embarrassing, but, although

Forbes acted the gentleman, he did warn me, in a round about way, that if I didn't stick to the riding-accident story, to explain my absence, there might be . . . some difficulty about me . . . leaving.'

She paused, reached across and squeezed his nearer hand with hers. 'I'm not really sure what it's all about, but it's something to do with you, isn't it?'

'Slow down a little and I'll tell you what's happened. You'll soon see Rawley Forbes is no gentleman.'

She listened in silence while he told her about witnessing Forbes shoot some unknown man. He could see how tense she was now, shaken by his details. . . .

'I suspected that note the Jenner boy brought me because it was printed, even though *you* sometimes do print instead of writing it out: you always say you're such a bad writer of longhand. . . .'

'Yeah. Forbes *was* the one I saw kill that other man, no doubt in my mind about that, despite his getting all barbered and changing his clothes. That was just to confuse things and raise a doubt. Which he has done. I told the sheriff I'd made a mistake . . . but I lied.'

'Because Forbes had me in his – custody?'

'Yeah, and McLaren's not happy. He knows something pressured me into trying to convince him about me not being sure it was Forbes.'

'If – if you hadn't changed your mind about identifying him what d'you think would've happened?'

'Don't worry about, it. It didn't happen and it won't.'

'You're not really changing your story, are you?'

'I know what I saw, and Forbes is gonna pay – more than ever, now. He won't get his hands on you again.'

'Clint, they didn't harm me. Two of Forbes's men were waiting when I crossed the river and my horse did stumble getting out, and sort of . . . threw me over its head. They might've crowded it just a little too much, but they said Forbes wanted to see me, anyway. So I went with them and there was a lot of round-about talk of what *might* happen to you if you insisted on telling what Forbes called lousy lies about him. He was hinting about court cases and the like, but I think I read between the lines correctly.' She gave a small shiver. 'I was afraid to think about what might happen to you and decided it was easier to comply than resist.'

'Yeah, I can savvy that.' His voice was tight and she reached over to squeeze his hand again. 'I went along with his game, too, so you wouldn't be harmed, but now you're out of his hands—'

'Clint, no! Please! Don't – don't put yourself in danger!'

'It's you who'll be in danger – and that I won't stand for. *Belle*! You know how I am about such things! I'll go along partway with Forbes now and admit he doesn't look a whole helluva lot like the man I saw murder the other one, with his fancy clothes and havin' a haircut and a shave. But I *know* damn well it was him, so he's got to pay. No matter what.'

They rode in silence for almost a mile before she

59

said, 'I know, and it *is* the right thing to do. Clint, I'm not afraid to stand up with you and—'

'Well, you've got to act as if you are. Dammit, Belle! Can't you see he's going to use you in any way he can to make me keep my mouth shut? I wish I *could* do it so you won't be bothered, but—'

'Don't you dare go back on your principles, not for me or anything else. It's one of your great strengths, Clint. I've always admired it, as many other people do. I know it might be dangerous, but if you're sure he did that brutal killing – well, he can't be allowed to get away with it.' She paused. 'You have no idea who the victim might be?'

'None. But it hardly matters. *A man was murdered,* so someone has to pay for it. We know who, and it just has to be done. I think you ought to visit your sister in Tucson for a couple of weeks until—'

'You think wrong, Clinton Reid. It'll be rough, perhaps, but I will stand beside you all the way. Now don't argue with me. Or . . . or I'll cancel our wedding plans.'

'Holy smoke!' He clapped a hand overdramatically, to his head. 'The wedding! I forgot all about the wedding. What are the plans again?'

'Oh, you darn fool!' She gave him a light tap on the jaw with a small, loosely clenched fist.

There was time for a brief, intense hug and an even briefer kiss, and then he said, 'No more jokes. I'll get this done as quickly and as safely as I can. Then we'll discuss weddings a bit more seriously.'

*

At Rocking C, he gave Mitch Camden a brief outline of what was happening. Mitch was a man who didn't like to 'get involved in things', as he called it, but Clint gave him enough details to make his eyes widen.

'Good Lord! You have to bring Forbes to justice, Clinton.' He never used the diminutive of Reid's name. 'But only if you are absolutely *certain* he's the man you saw commit that murder. There's no room for mistakes.'

'I'm sure. Why else would Forbes go through all this act with Belle? He's really showing me he can reach her whenever he wants and he'll use her to press me into withdrawing my accusation about him.'

'You . . . do you want a couple of my men to act as sort of . . . bodyguards for Belle? I can spare them.'

'That's *my* job, Mitch. But it wouldn't hurt to keep an eye on her. Make sure she doesn't ride alone, 'specially out of sight of the house.'

Mitch Camden looked at him squarely and after a moment nodded. 'Yes, I believe you are capable of taking care of my sister, Clint, but should you need help. . . .'

'Thanks. I'll remember.'

She came with him when he was preparing to leave, watched him saddle his horse. When he'd done so, she went to stand by him.

'Clint, Rawley Forbes didn't really fool me with his gentlemanly attentions and all his double-talk about you having mistakenly identified him as the killer, you know. I went along with him because he's a very

61

dangerous man, so please be careful, *very* careful.'

'My middle name. Belle, it might be best if you stick close to the house here, don't ride near any boundaries or talk to any strangers.'

'Yes, *Father*!' She answered him with a cheeky grin. She punched him lightly on the shoulder. 'Don't worry so much about me. I can take care of myself.'

'Just take this seriously, Belle. Forbes has a helluva lot to lose – his whole damn life! He's not going to pull any punches to make sure that doesn't happen.'

'Then *you*'re the one who must be careful.' She stepped forward and put her arms about him. 'Please, Clint?'

'I swear it on our wedding rings – or I will when I can afford to buy them.'

'Oh!' she said with a touch of exasperation, almost stamping her foot, but instead she tightened her arms about him.

He responded, but his concern was genuine: it had been so damn easy for Forbes to get her in his clutches.

And that was with the mildest of warnings.

If he really wanted to apply pressure to Reid . . . well, Clint didn't want to think about what the man might do.

But he knew for sure that someone else would die before this thing was over.

He just had to make damned sure it wasn't Belle. Or himself.

CHAPTER 6

BEST-LAID PLANS

Reid had plenty of chores to do around the ranch. Not that it was particularly large, or that the terrain was all that difficult, but he was working it alone.

Usually when he had any problems that needed another hand – or two or three – he looked no further than the Rocking C. Mitch Camden would willingly supply the extra men to help out with the really difficult jobs.

Clint appreciated this. Mitch would normally refuse any kind of payment, but Reid would slip the men who had helped him a couple of dollars on the quiet.

'Up to you, Clinton,' Mitch would say. 'But, far as I'm concerned, you're family, or near enough to it, and that entitles you to ask for whatever you need. Except money. I don't believe in lending money or giving it for frivolous things.'

Once he quietly added, by way of some sort of explanation: 'Belle was too young at the time to remember, but our father "borrowed" money from a neighbouring big rancher – this was back in Arizona – who told him: "No hurry to pay it back, Lew. Just when you can." Which sounded fine, except he didn't say the loan was accumulating interest all the time. When he felt like it, why, he simply walked in and took over our ranch and pointed the whole family in the direction of the nearest horizon. "You're a good worker, Lew Camden," he said. "Go and build yourself another ranch." Of course it never happened and the family broke up, scattered. Had to. Each had to find his or her own way. Still dunno what happened to two of our brothers. I took it on myself to look out for Belle, but I'm happy for her to marry you, Clinton. I'll help all I can; just don't ask for money.'

'No intention of doing so,' Clint had told him, just a mite stiffly. 'I'm a man likes to pay his own way.'

'I know. One of the things I like about you. Between the two of us we'll see no harm comes to Belle.'

'Damn right!'

Even so, Clint Reid couldn't rest easy; he worried about Belle constantly, knowing the kind of man Rawley Forbes was. No scruples; a liar; and the only person in the world the man worried about was himself: Rawley Forbes, murderer. Clint also worried about that part: no matter what, the fact was Forbes did murder that unknown man – and he was getting away with it by his threats to Belle, thus tying Reid's hands. And it just wasn't right.

But he had to live with it, for now, at least. . . .

He was building a small log dam across the creek that ran through his land. It wasn't an urgent project, but one he wanted to finish before winter set in. Using the natural fall of the land, he would be able to run water down to pasture where he would keep his small but growing herd. It would save a lot of time if he dug another channel to use for allowing some of the water from the dam to spread out on the flats, nourishing the grass for the future.

It was innovative enough for some of the smaller local ranchers to ride over and see how he was pro-gressing. Some helped with the excavations and Reid promised that when complete – and providing his own herds were catered for – the neighbours could make use of the channel to water portions of their own herds.

It made him popular and men from the high country rode down and spent a day or two studying his layout, hoping they would be able to adapt Clint's ideas for Buckshot Ridge to their own elevated pas-tures.

So there were riders coming and going most days, and seeing a horseman on the ridge or riding along the crest was distracting. Once or twice Clint had seen the flash of sun on the lenses of field glasses as someone studied his methods, but mainly those interested came riding down to ask him questions, make notes or draw rough sketches.

Still, having all these riders in the vicinity only added to his worries: he had to check each and every one to make sure they were bona fide and not scouting for Forbes.

'Hoping to make enough from the first market drive to buy a windmill,' Clint confessed to a couple of interested neighbours. 'Save digging, and I can pump the water uphill. I get a pretty steady norther coming right smack down the middle of my ridge, so I'm crossing my fingers.'

Mitch Camden, of course, was very interested and rode across often, accompanied by Belle. She was looking healthy now the cooler weather was coming and Clint felt his heart actually do a somersault – he swore it was so a few times when he sighted her coming through the short but winding pass between the two spreads.

'You sure are a beauty, Belle,' he told her one time. 'I still dunno how come you agreed to marry me.'

'Oh, well, I thought it was time. I was sure I was going to end up an old maid, so when you stumbled and hemmed and hawed and finally got out your proposal, I thought I'd better grab with both hands or I *will* end up an old maid.'

'Ah! So that's it. You were desperate and I walked right into it.'

'Exactly! I've had a couple of second thoughts but, as you say, I was desperate. But I think it'll work out.'

'Sounds like interesting times, coming up.'

She stepped closer to him, locking her fingers through his on his right hand, tugging him closer, then rose on her toes and kissed him. 'Very interesting – or I'll want to know why not.'

He glanced around, turning, shading his eyes, until she asked what on earth he was doing.

'Just thinkin'. If I hadn't done so much work on the ranch I might just ride away from it all. I'm feelin' kinda . . . nervous now. Might even say . . . scared.'

She laughed. 'You ride away and I'll follow.'

'Threat or promise?'

'I'll *follow*. Depend on it.'

'Hmm. Might's well stick around, then.'

'You'd better!'

They laughed and it felt like a good, natural thing to do. It was a time – brief though it was – of happiness.

But, as so often happens, it couldn't last.

It started when Sheriff McLaren sent a message saying he'd like to see Clint Reid in his office. Any time, but sooner the better.

'You want to ride into town with me?' Clint asked Belle, who was up to her elbows in flour and sugar and other cake ingredients in Mitch's kitchen.

She brushed some of her hair back, leaving a smear of flour on her forehead.

'Oh, Clint, I wish you'd asked me earlier. I can't leave the cake at this stage.' She lowered her voice, glanced at the kitchen doorway and said, 'It's Mitch's birthday and I wanted to surprise him. I need to get the cake into the oven as soon as possible. You couldn't leave your town visit until tomorrow I suppose?'

'Guess not. McLaren sent word he wants to see me – he didn't say, but I just have a feeling it's important.'

'I'm sorry, Clint. Such a beautiful day for a ride.'

'OK. You're off the hook. Providing I get an invite to the party.'

She grinned through the floury smears. 'Not exactly a party, but . . . well, it's an idea. We could all do with some relaxation.'

He kissed her briefly, put on his hat and made for the door. 'I'll come over when I get back from town.'

'Good. Oh, could you bring back some tobacco? I've bought Mitch a new pipe.'

'When'd you get that?' he asked sharply.

'Oh, the other day when you were busy with Eric Carson and his men on your new channel. I rode in and—'

'Dammit, Belle!' He gripped her arm tightly but eased his hold as soon as she grimaced. 'God*damit*! I've told you you're never to go riding anywhere unless I'm with you. Or Mitch, or some of his men. You can't trust Forbes. He's been mighty quiet, but it doesn't mean it's safe for you to ride anywhere you please.'

'Clint! I'm not a baby. In fact, I'm a year or two older than you. And I took a short cut, anyway: the trail that goes *behind* the range, so I entered town from another direction.'

He shook his head sharply. 'The worst possible thing to do. Out of sight of everyone who could help you should you need it. Come on, Belle, I lose hours of sleep worrying about your safety and then you go and do something plain stupid like this.'

'Who're you calling "stupid"?' He saw the blaze of anger in her eyes and waited for the expected tirade, but she closed her mouth abruptly, studied him more closely. 'Clint, you worry too much about me. I *can* look after myself.'

'Not if Forbes wants you as a hostage. He knows it's the only way he can force me to keep my mouth shut. That, or the threat of doing it. Now, the sheriff's sent for me and he wouldn't do that unless there's been some kinda . . . development.'

'Then you'd better go and find out what it is. And if you'll get out of my way, I'll take this cake mix across to the oven and. . . .' She hustled by him, holding her anger with difficulty.

'I'll see you when I get back, then,' he said shortly. 'And what brand of tobacco. . . ?'

She looked at him, gently closed the oven door. 'The one with the old sailing ship on the label. I'm not sure what it's called. I'll pay you when you return.'

But he was already going through the door and her white teeth tugged at her lower lip: she knew he was right about the risk she had taken, but she couldn't stand being cooped up – or being bossed. It can't go on for ever, she told herself. . . .

Sheriff McLaren shuffled some papers as he looked at Clint Reid seated across the desk from him.

'I can't just let this rest, son. I know damn well – and you do, too – that you *saw* Rawley Forbes murder someone on that ridge.' He lifted a hand slightly as Clint started to say something. 'Belle, of course, is the weakness in the whole deal. Forbes gets his hands on her and he can make you jump through hoops.' He looked hard at Reid. 'Can't he?'

Clint nodded solemnly. 'Afraid so, Si.'

'Like he has already, with you sayin' you're not *sure* it was him you saw, just because he'd cleaned himself up a little, changed his clothes, and because he let you know how he could use Belle to bring you to heel.'

Reid looked uncomfortable. 'Look, Si, I'm sorry about backin' down, but he demonstrated just how easy it is for him to get Belle in his hands. Hell, don't you think I want to see the son of a bitch behind bars? Or dancing on a gallows?'

'I savvy all that, son. Don't blame you. But I've always done my job the best I can. And I ain't doin' my best by sittin' here, knowing Forbes is guilty and I'm not able to do one damn thing about it because I don't have a witness. Unless you change your mind. . . .'

'You know my position, Si. You guarantee Belle's safety at all – *all* – times and I'll rethink it.'

'You've got to be certain sure it was him who fired

70

those shots, say it in court, swear it on a Bible.'

Clint nodded. 'Hell, don't you think I know all that?' He had to bite back the really angry words he wanted to use. 'It gripes the hell outta me to have to sit and twiddle my thumbs, knowin' he's gonna get away with it.'

'*No – he – ain't*!'

Clint jumped when the old lawman roared the three words. It must have cost McLaren some effort, for he had a bout of coughing that Reid thought was never going to end.

'Judas! You all right?' Clint said, getting quickly to his feet. But McLaren waved him back as he reached for a crumpled kerchief in his hip pocket, coughed into it a few times, then wiped his mouth and settled back in his chair, chest heaving.

'I won't – let him – get away with this,' he rasped. 'I've waited years to get something on him and this is *it*! My health might be ailin', but I need your help to nail him, son, and I can't let the present situation drag on for much longer.' He reached into his desk drawer and brought out a couple of handwritten pages. 'This is your original statement and I've entered it officially in my files. So you'll have hell's own job tryin' to change it now. Copies've gone to the federal marshal's office in Medicine Bow, too, so you're officially on the records.'

'You didn't have to pull something like that.'

'Yeah, I did, son. I have to force your hand. Oh, don't think I ain't got a bad conscience about it. I know the danger it puts Belle in; once Forbes gets her you'll be in that well-known spot between a rock and a hard place.'

Clint's jaw was knotted and his eyes narrowed as he stared across the cluttered desk at the lawman.

'I've been there for some time now – ever since I got that note from Forbes when he had Belle at his place.'

'Yeah, Rawley made his point like I'm tryin' to make mine – now!'

'How we gonna protect Belle twenty-four hours a day? Sure, Mitch is her brother and he'll do his best, but he's kinda . . . naïve; he thinks by always doing the "right thing" that everything'll work out. Don't get me wrong. He's no fool, and he'll fight to protect Belle, but he hopes he won't need to fight.'

The lawman thought about it, slowly nodded. 'That's as maybe, but it don't alter anythin', son. This is my last term wearin' this badge, health's goin' and I'm feelin' my age, but I aim to finish it on a high note. You waverin' back and forth about whether it *was* Forbes you saw or not ain't helpin' a whole helluva lot. 'Specially when we both know damn well it *was* Rawley Forbes you saw.'

Clint felt his cheeks burn a little, nodded slowly.

'I want to nail him as bad as you – but I can't risk Belle's life to do it – and I won't.'

'You sleep all right, son?'

'I've had a few restless nights lately, I admit.'

'Conscience.'

'Damn you, McLaren!'

'See? You're rarin' to go with this. I don't have

deputies I can send to watch out for Belle, but Mitch should be able to rustle up two or three of his cowhands to watch her. You think of that?'

'Yeah, I have. Mitch'd do whatever's necessary. Probably sit there with a loaded shotgun himself.'

'Then you'll do it? You'll forget this eyewash about not being certain whether it was Forbes you saw murder that feller? I can't fangdangle that . . . crap any longer. We've gotta make a move. Get – it – done!'

'When I'm certain-sure Belle will be *safe* at all times, McLaren, and only then.' Clint sounded stubborn.

'Good enough. Why don't we ride out together, mebbe stop at Mitch Camden's on the way and see if he'd like to come along and bring a couple men. Huh?'

Clint smiled slowly. 'You're a careful man, McLaren, but I'm with you.'

'Uh-huh.' The old sheriff grunted a couple of times as he got out of his chair. 'Then, after we arrest Forbes on suspicion, all we gotta do is find the body.'

Reid frowned. 'Mebbe that should be done first?'

'Ideally, yeah, I agree. But what I want to do is kinda undermine Forbes's confidence and legally hold him in my cells on suspicion, where I can tie him up with more legal mumbo-jumbo than he can shake a stick at while I do this and check that, get papers away to the federal marshals, and wait for 'em to get back to me. Just might wear him down a mite.'

'The idea's OK. Provided the body is under all that dirt.'

'Oh, I reckon it is. And the longer we take with all the legal work, the more nervous Forbes'll get and mebbe let somethin' slip or do somethin' desperate.'

Clint looked uncertain. 'It's not a sure method, Si. What if he brings in a bunch of lawyers?'

Si McLaren sat back in his chair and looked sour.

'Yeah. That's one big flaw in my plan. Pity, ain't it?'

'By hell it is! You want my honest opinion, Sheriff, I don't think it's gonna work. He's got us.'

McLaren tapped his horny-nailed fingers on the desk, the old rheumy eyes boring into Clint.

'Or thinks he has – but there's somethin' else, too. You ever think that the easiest thing for him to do, to shake the whole damn hassle, get rid of it completely – is to kill *you*? You're his biggest threat – the eye-witness. You die an' his problem goes away.'

Clint's face told the sheriff that he had thought of that, and the fact that he had, and still went along with his silence, showed how much he cared about Belle, and keeping her out of harm's way.

'It's sort of gettin' to you, son? I mean, man like you – it must really roast you, *knowin'* Forbes is the killer and yet you have to keep it to yourself, or you lose Belle.'

A frown leapt across Clint's face. 'By hell! You think anything – anything in the whole damn world – would save Forbes then? But I'd never let it get that far, Si. And I don't thank you a helluva lot for making me think about it. You schemin' old son of a bitch!'

The sheriff did his best to look contrite but he was inwardly smiling: he'd succeeded in stirring up Reid to the point where something would be done to end this stalemate.

But, more than likely, someone would die in the process.

CHAPTER 7

BLAME

Clint Reid was still annoyed that Belle had taken such a risk by riding into town for a pipe for Mitch's birthday.

He was more angry at himself than anything, but rationalized by convincing himself he had a lot to do and a lot on his mind.

'Surely, Mitch, with a ranch crew at your disposal, you could put someone on full-time to keep an eye on her?'

That's what he told his future brother-in-law when he saw Mitch in town at the cattle agency. 'You've gotta be more alert where Belle's concerned, Mitch.'

'Listen, Clinton, she's my sister! We grew up together, had the usual family tiffs and so on. She's headstrong if you try to restrict her too much. I know this is dangerous and she could be at risk from Forbes, but ... well, all right, I guess mebbe I

76

could've been a little more watchful when you get right down to it. Dammit, man! I've got a ranch to run, too. Bigger than your one-man outfit. I can't think of everything. But – yeah, I'll keep a closer eye on her. Nothing happened, so you don't need to ride me.'

'I think I needed to, Mitch. Sorry, but that's the way I feel. I love your sister and this being on tenterhooks night and day makes me edgy. If I offended you it wasn't intentional, but you've gotten my message, so. . . .' He thrust out his right hand. 'OK?'

Mitch, to his credit, didn't hesitate: they shook hands and the older rancher smiled slowly. 'She always won our arguments, you know. Right from when we were just youngsters.'

'Got that way about her,' admitted Clint, smiling too. 'This damn thing with Forbes has got to be settled. Si's doing his best, but – hate to say it – I think his best was a long time ago. He's just a mite too old, has had it easy and he's kinda outta his depth now he's got something serious to handle. His health's goin', too.'

'Yeah, I'd go along with that. He's a good man and he's had a long run, but he's slowed down. Don't worry about Belle. I'll have a man keep an eye on her full-time.'

'Thanks, Mitch. Say, I still haven't found that damn heifer I was chasin' when I saw Forbes kill that feller. It might try to join your herds, so could you keep an eye out, just in case? That's if the wolves haven't already got to it.'

'Charley West was ridin' line yesterday and he said he thought he saw a stray heifer. Over to the bluff above the river bend, just outside our line. It ran off, though, before he could get a rope on it. Could be the one you're after.'

'Might be. I'll take a look. Thanks, and *adios*.'

That afternoon, Belle was still tense and decided to exercise her favourite sorrel: see if a ride would settle her down a little, and she'd give Mitch his present at the same time.

Mitch had just completed a castrating session and was washing up when she found him. He dried his hair, buttoned his shirt and was mighty pleased with the new pipe she had bought him, along with the wallet of Clipper tobacco. But he took her aside and gave her a stern talking-to about leaving the ranch's confines without an escort.

'Darn it, Mitch! I hate all these precautions,' she said edgily. 'Oh, I know they're necessary but I – I'd like to get my hands around Rawley Forbes's neck and *squeeze*.'

He rubbed his own neck briefly and gave her a crooked smile. 'I can still feel those hands that time you got to me that way. Thought I was a goner!'

'Do you blame me? When you'd loosened my cinchstrap and then told me Dad wanted me up at the house urgently – and I ended up in a mud puddle. If he hadn't come along I think I just might've throttled you.'

He nodded. 'I thought so, too. But Clinton's right,

sis. You have to be more careful. I'm going to Si McLaren to find out what can be done. None of us want to go on like this for much longer.'

She nodded curtly. 'No. But Clint was . . . well, kinda rough on me. I think he might be still sore at me.'

'Now, look, he had a right. Just settle down and try to realize no one's bossin' you around for the fun of it. We've all got your best interests at heart.'

Her brother's words gave her pause. Yes, she supposed she was being – childish – though she hated to admit it. Everyone was looking out for her and here she was getting her dander up.

'How stupid can you get?' she asked herself. 'I'll have to try to make things up to Clint for my behaviour. But how?' A moment later she had the answer. 'Of course!'

She hurried outside and called one of the cowboys working at the big pump. 'Len, where's Charley West?'

'Down by the river, Belle. Couple of yearlin's were bogged but I think they're free now. I can ride down and fetch him, if you want.'

'No, it's all right, Len. I'll go see him myself.'

'Er – Mitch says you gotta have someone watchin' out for you if you go ridin' anywhere.'

'Darn it, Len! I can watch out for myself. You tell my brother that if he asks. No! Don't argue with me. Just cut out my horse while I change, please.'

Len hesitated, but – well, she was the boss's sister.

'Whatever you say, Belle.'

Riding well beyond the big bend of the river, she heard a couple of gunshots: a rifle, she decided.

It had to be Charley: no other ranch hands were working in this vicinity according to Mitch.

She found him stretched out on a small rise, lying on one side as he reloaded his rifle. He jumped when she rode up, swinging the weapon down, but relaxed when he saw who it was. He got hurriedly to his feet. He was a man in his mid-twenties, deferential to the boss's sister, at the same time wondering why the hell she was here.

'Afternoon, Belle. Just been trackin' a couple wolves that were stakin' out that small pasture yonder. Got 'em both.'

'Nice shooting, Charley. Past all that brush, too.'

Her words relaxed him and he felt a mite embarrassed. 'Always been pretty good with a rifle. Can I help you?'

She told him she was looking for Clint's escaped heifer. 'I know he didn't recover it but it's one he wants to breed from eventually. Have you seen any sign of it?'

'Had a glimpse of one before I nailed those wolves. They could've been trackin' it. Sort of a buckskin colour.'

'That sounds like it. He favoured it because of the colour of the hide. Where did you see it?'

He gestured beyond the patch of brush where he had shot the wolves. 'On the slope above. Them wolves were sniffin' around, so it's lucky I spotted 'em. Dunno if it's still up there. But there won't be no wolves – I guarantee that.'

She smiled slowly: that was four or five times Charley had mentioned his victory over the lobos.

'Well, I'll tell Mitch you're doing a fine job, Charley.'

'Thanks, ma'am.' *Message received*, he decided.

'Can you come with me? Help me track the heifer down?'

Charley felt a little jump in his stomach: *the boss's sister asking him to help her?*

'Why, sure, ma'am – Belle. It'll be my pleasure.'

'You don't think some wolves may've got it yet?' she asked, kind of slyly, but Charley didn't notice.

'Well, sure not them two I just shot. But I never seen any more tracks over this way. Most seem to be across t'other side of the river. But I'll ride ahead, if you like, and if I find they have been at the heifer – well, I'll come back and tell you, so you don't have to see the – the mess.'

'That's thoughtful of you, Charley. Can we go now?'

'Yes, *ma'am*!'

The brush was reasonably heavy and they had to detour around a couple of places, passing the carcasses of the two wolves Charley had shot. He hesitated, then pointed out to her that he had hit both just behind the left foreleg.

'Right through the ticker, both times. They never suffered none, if you was wonderin'.'

'You're a very good rifle shot, Charley,' she told him, urging her horse on, hoping that was the last she would hear about the damn wolves he had shot.

Charley's mount suddenly swerved and reared, and he had to tussle with the reins and then free one hand to snatch at the saddle horn. At the same time Belle heard the crash of a gunshot close by. A bullet creased Charley's mount's neck and the horse went down, taking him with it. He tried to throw himself clear but wasn't quite quick enough and his right leg was pinned, foot jammed in the stirrup. It was also the side he wore his six-gun and, lying on it now, he couldn't reach it.

Belle's horse reared and whinnied in fright, but she managed to bring it down on an even keel, and she instinctively leaned forward in the saddle to pat the mount's neck, soothing it even as she looked around.

There was a man standing by a clump of boulders, levering a fresh cartridge into his smoking rifle.

'Take it easy, Charley, and I won't have to shoot you,' he said, and as he turned his face to the sunlight she recognized Hank Purcell. He smiled crookedly, jerking the rifle barrel. 'Settle that bronc, woman! I got no urge to shoot it out from under you, but I won't hesitate if you don't quiet it down. That's better, much better. Now, come to Poppa an' make me happy.'

She glanced towards Charley West as he started to struggle again and gasped as Hank Purcell walked his mount across and halted it beside Charley.

'I'd just as soon shoot you, Charley. I ain't forgot that fight we had in town – when was it? Last Christmas? Nope. Wasn't no snow so it musta been – goddammit, will you stop tryin' to get at your gun!'

He suddenly yelled as Charley West managed to force his right hand between his body and the ground and actually touch his gun butt.

Then Hank shot him.

The girl gave a cry of alarm, and her horse jumped, so she had a few intensely busy moments calming it down. Wide-eyed, she looked down at Charley, who was writhing as much as he could, under the panicky horse, his right shoulder a bloody mess from Hank Purcell's bullet.

His mount continued bucking and struggling, lurched awkwardly to its feet, and Charley's boot slipped out of the stirrup as the animal trotted off twenty paces or so before stopping and turning to look back to where its master lay groaning, its ears pricked.

'Quit the big act, Charley,' Purcell told him, still holding his smoking Colt. 'It'll hurt for a spell but you'll live, so you get yourself together, climb on to your hoss, and ride on back to Mitch. Tell him if he wants to see his sister again, in reasonable condition, he better make sure Clint Reid has a total loss of memory. He'll know what I mean. Hold it, you bitch! Or I'll shoot you instead of your hoss!'

Belle reined up sharply at the command, breathing hard; she turned in the saddle to see that Hank had his gun pointed in her direction. She lifted her

83

hands slowly, level with her shoulders.

'Let me at least bandage Charley's shoulder,' she said, annoyed that her voice trembled.

'Just stay put. He ain't hurt bad. Tougher than old boots, ain't that right, Charley?'

'Next – next time we – have a fight – it'll be with – guns – not – just fists, Hank.'

'OK! Fine with me. Aw, all right, woman, he's bleedin' a mite worse than I figured. Bind the wound with his neckerchief, then get back in your saddle. You try anythin' else and I'll kill Charley and find some other way to get word to Clint Reid that you won't be back home for a spell.'

Belle froze. She knew Hank Purcell's reputation for meanness. But she was darned if she was just going to do what he wanted! The trouble was, she let this decision show on her face and in the haughty angle of her jaw as she looked at him coldly.

He stared back, smiling. 'That's OK. Fight me all you want. Reckon I might even enjoy it. You game?'

Her breath hissed through pinched nostrils and she clasped her hands tightly, hoping her voice would be steady when she spoke.

'You get rough with me, Hank Purcell, and my brother or Clint Reid will kill you.'

Purcell smiled crookedly. 'Sure they will. Or they'll try. Won't do you a lotta good, though, either way, will it?' He pouted his lips suddenly and made a sucking sound that sent shivers down her spine.

'Damn you, Hank!' gritted Charley West.

'Aw, shut *up*, Charley.' He strode across and kicked

the cowboy in the side of the head, hard enough to jerk the man's body a few inches through the gravel.

Belle gasped, a hand going to her mouth. 'Stop it! You'll kill him.'

'Mmm. Mebbe a little later. First I can use him.' He leaned over the moaning Charley, then straightened, nodding to himself. 'Gotta head like a cannonball. He'll be OK, an' he'll deliver my message. Meantime, you an' me can get a mite more cosy while I take you back to see Rawley. You know, I got a notion that Rawley kinda fancies you.'

Belle felt the tearing pit of raw fear surge through her.

Not only the *idea* of Forbes 'fancying' her, but here she was at his mercy – actually, Hank Purcell's mercy – but he was acting on Forbes's behalf.

She felt that trickle of real, genuine fear: the awful, terrifying kind that seemed to paralyze her with the knowledge that there was nothing she could do.

CHAPTER 8

ENOUGH IS ENOUGH!

Flapjack, Mitch Camden's cook, grunted as he straightened from dressing Charley West's shoulder wound. The injured man rolled his head, moaning in semi-conscious pain.

The cook had a head of unruly, faded brown hair shot through with a few streaks of grey. He pushed it back from his stubbled face as he looked at Mitch Camden.

'Best I can do, Mitch. He's not gonna be able to work for a long time. That bullet nicked his collar-bone as well as messin' up a lot of tendons. Could be he ... well, he might not be much good as a cowhand from here on in.'

Mitch, not a man usually given to much cussing, let go with a stream of blistering words that should

have totally annihilated Rawley Forbes and his ances-
tors.

He paced jerkily across the room and back,
looking down at Charley.

'If you think he needs a sawbones, either take him
into town in a buckboard, or send someone to bring
the doc out here. Just to make sure.'

Flapjack's face straightened a little. 'I reckon I've
done all Doc Daybright could do, Mitch,' he said,
rather stiffly, and the rancher waved a hand irritably.

'Not criticizing your work, Flapjack. But Charley's
a damn good hand and I don't want him crippled
just because a proper doctor might know that little
bit more from his years of medical experience. Your
work's always fine with me and the boys, but we
haven't had a shattered shoulder before, if my
memory serves. Sure not one like this.'

'No-o-o. Not as bad as this. Well, I wouldn't want to
see ol' Charley crippled just because I got a mite
touchy, boss. Sorry. Got me a leetle bit of a hangover.'

'Well, you just take care of Charley and we'll all
wait for our supper if we have to. Give him priority,
OK?'

Flapjack nodded a mite glumly and leaned down
when Charley West opened his reddened eyes.

'Where. . . ? Aw, it's you, you old grubspoiler.'

Flapjack's mouth tightened and he looked coldly
at the rancher. 'That's the thanks I get.'

'You did a fine job, Flapjack,' Mitch said quickly,
frowning a little as he turned to the wounded man.
'Charley, who was it shot you?'

87

'Goddamn Hank Purcell! Orders from Forbes. He reckons . . . m-message for you – about – Miss Belle.'

Mitch Camden tensed, leaned closer. 'Which is. . . ?'

'She'll be stayin' with him – for a spell. She – she'll be – all right – long as – as Clint completely forgets what he saw, or what he *says* he saw, is how Forbes put it.'

'That part's to be expected,' the rancher said sourly. 'And if Clint *doesn't* withdraw his accusation. . . ?'

'He – din' go into – de – details, but – he made it plain enough. You – you mightn't – recognize Miss Belle if an' when – he does send her back.'

'*Christ!* Who the hell does he think he is that he could get away with something like that?'

'Dunno, boss, but he sure scared the hell outta me. He means what he says.'

'So do I. When I say I'm going to see about this I mean *see about it.* No more pussyfooting. Enough's enough. Forbes wants to play rough, that – suits – me.'

Mitch Camden sent a messenger for Clint Reid to come see him – pronto.

Clint arrived, grim-faced, six-gun on his right hip, scabbarded rifle in his hands.

'Don't keep me long, Mitch.'

'Don't intend to. Obviously you know the latest development.'

'I know that son of a bitch Forbes has Belle.'

'Because of you.' Mitch Camden said, unsmiling.

'Now, wait a minute—'

'You wait. But not too damn long! You know what Forbes wants. Now you do it – or you'll answer to me.'

Clint looked soberly at the irate rancher. 'Just forget I saw Forbes murder a man in cold blood? It ain't that easy, Mitch.'

'Then *make* it that easy. Goddammit, Clinton! It's Belle's *well-being* on the line here – I'd go so far as to say her life. Now, you've got the power to stop this and I'm askin' you to do so!'

Clint shook his head slowly, then tensed when Mitch dropped a hand to his gun butt.

'Whoa! For Chrissakes, Mitch! Get this in perspective.'

'I have. You saw somethin' that could put Rawley Forbes behind bars for the rest of his life. Or he could even be hung. You keep quiet about it long enough for us to get Belle back, then we double-cross the son of a bitch and go after him. All out! No punches pulled. We kill him. And do the whole damn world a favour. OK?'

Clint held the cold stare for a long moment, Mitch's face was very flushed. '*O-kay*, I said.' snapped the rancher.

'Not OK, Mitch. *Wait*, goddammit! *Think*, man. You'd never get near Forbes with his string of hard-cases, for one thing. And the other is somethin' you've obviously forgotten.'

'What's that?' Mitch asked through gritted teeth.

'Si McLaren.'

Mitch blinked. 'Si. . . ? What the hell! I'm not worried about that old fool. Should've pensioned him off long ago.'

'But he's still the official sheriff of this county and he's determined to nail Forbes's hide to the wall. And that's even if he has to die doing it. It's become an obsession with him.'

Mitch looked his disbelief. 'Old Si? You're dreaming, Clint. He's a has-been. He can't handle somethin' like this. And I'm damned if I'm gonna wait for him to make up his mind just what he's gonna do. Belle's my sister and, in case you've overlooked it, your bride-to-be.'

He shook his head violently. 'I don't understand your attitude, boy. Fact, I don't think I'd want you in the Camden family – by marriage or any other way if you don't stir yourself.'

That startled Clint some and he was silent longer than he intended.

As Mitch opened his mouth to speak again, Clint said: 'Belle's over twenty-one, Mitch. It's up to her who she chooses for a husband. You've got no say in that.'

'The hell I ain't!' Mitch slapped his hand to his gun butt and his mouth froze in the half-open position as he blinked, and stared down the muzzle of Clint Reid's Colt, steady in his hand and the hammer cocked. Mitch's breath whistled through his teeth.

'Jeee-sus! Where – where the hell you learn to draw like that, boy?'

'Guess mebbe it comes naturally. Now, let's keep some sanity in this, Mitch. Just stop stewin' for a minute and try to savvy the situation. The point is, like it or not, Rawley Forbes holds all the cards.'

Mitch frowned, then grudgingly said, 'Right now.'

'Yeah, *right now.* What we have to do is figure a way to make him drop 'em without Belle gettin' hurt.'

Mitch stared back, then added quietly: '*And* you. OK, I got a bit overexcited there, but I tell you, Clinton, I'm all shook up. And I'm damn sure we won't get any help from Si McLaren.'

'I think we just might. But we've got to handle it mighty carefully or we're both going to be in mourning for Belle.'

Mitch glared. 'Judas! You sure got a way of – of puttin' a man at ease.'

Clint smiled crookedly. 'Lack of practice. Now, let's go see the sheriff – together. After we see Forbes. All right?'

Mitch nodded jerkily and holstered his gun. His breath hissed audibly through his pinched nostrils when, after a brief hesitation, Clint slid his Colt back into leather also.

Rawley Forbes, hair combed back and parted neatly enough, his clothes clean, though they could do with ironing, Mitch Camden thought, stepped out on to his porch and bent his head to touch a burning match to his cheroot. He shook out the flame and flicked the dead vesta away over the rail, smiled with a nod, looking a mite puzzled. He ran his eyes over

91

his visitors: Clint Reid and Mitch Camden, and Sheriff Si McLaren, who looked mighty tired beneath his grimness.

'Well, gents, this is a surprise. I don't usually get visitors in a group, but welcome, Now, what can I do for you?'

Mitch beat Clint's reply by a split second.

'We're here to see Belle. And don't try to tell us she ain't here.'

'Why would I do that? Yeah, Belle's here for a few days. She . . . well, ask her yourself.' He raised his voice. 'Belle. You got visitors.' He smiled at the trio. 'You are *her* visitors, rather than mine, am I right?'

'*Damn* right!' said Mitch curtly.

Belle appeared in the doorway, stopped in her tracks when she saw the three riders.

Then her face lit up with a bright smile. 'My! What a pleasant surprise! Clint, Mitch – and hello to you, too, Sheriff McLaren. I certainly wasn't expecting to see you.'

'Me neither,' said Forbes drily. 'But come sit you down, gents, and I'll have someone bring you a cold drink.'

'We'll do our talkin' from here,' the lawman said curtly, swinging his rheumy eyes to the girl. 'You all right, Miss Belle?'

She looked surprised, glanced at the equally puzzled-looking Forbes and smiled again.

'Of course I'm all right, Sheriff. Why wouldn't I be?'

The trio exchanged glances and Clint and Mitch

both sat straighter in their saddles. It was Clint who replied.

'We were given to understand, Belle, that you were brought here – possibly against your will.'

'Good heavens! What gave you that idea? No, no, you're mistaken. I was riding with Charley West out by the river bend and he went after some wolves he thought might bother the herds and there was an . . . accident.'

'What kinda "accident"?' wheezed old Si McLaren, scepticism apparent in his tone.

'I'm not sure. But he fell, or dropped his rifle, or something, and it went off and shot him in the shoulder. Rawley and Hank Purcell were near by and came across. They gave Charley first aid – he was acting a little strange. . . .'

'My guess is it was probably the shock,' put in Forbes, deadpan, but no one else made a comment.

'Anyway, to cut a long story short, Hank was sent to escort Charley to within sight of your ranch house, Mitch, and then Rawley told me he'd uncovered some antique furniture he'd been storing and we'd spoken about last time I was here, and would I like to see it? I said, "Yes", of course.'

'*Antique – furniture?*' echoed Clint. 'Since when've you been interested in antique furniture, for God's sake?'

'Oh, I've always been interested in it, haven't I, Mitch?'

Mitch Camden frowned. 'Well, I know you always liked that old furniture Uncle Terry and Aunt Cora

93

had, but—'

'See?' she cut in, still with that fixed smile. 'I've been going to surprise you, Clint, and have our house filled with genuine old tables and chairs and – and a bed and – so on. Something – elegant.'

Her smile faded a little: she had plucked to pieces a lace handkerchief she had been holding, without being aware of it. Belle fixed Clint with a steady, probing – *appealing?* – stare.

'Well, that would've been a surprise, all right,' Clint stammered haltingly. 'You want to start back now? Be sundown before we get home.'

Before she could answer, Forbes spoke, amiably enough: 'I've already arranged for Belle to stay over tonight – if she wishes, of course; in fact our meal's being cooked right now. You see, I've got the boys unpacking some crates of chairs and small tables I've kept all these years. Belle said she'd like to see them, maybe buy 'em. So, you gents can be on your way, if you like, and I'll see Belle's well fed and – er – taken care of for the night. I'll escort her home myself in the morning – after she's looked at the chairs—'

'Now wait up,' snapped Mitch, who had been looking grimmer and grimmer as the conversation continued. 'Belle's stayin' with me and—'

'Not for tonight, Mitch,' cut in Forbes, pleasantly. 'My Spanish cook has gone to a lot of trouble and—'

'Oh, yes, she really has,' Belle agreed, with that strange breathlessness in her voice again, as she looked at Clint Reid. 'I'm sure she'd be insulted if I

94

walked out on her now.'

'I brought Conchita all the way up from Juárez, had to pay her parents a slew of cash, and – well, she's volatile. And I'd rather not have the hassle, gents,' Forbes put in, looking and sounding genuinely worried.

Clint saw both Si and Mitch working up sharp retorts and said, 'Well, I guess one night won't hurt. But I'll come over myself in the morning and bring her home. OK, Belle?'

She threw a quick glance towards Forbes, who shrugged. 'You mightn't be able to inspect that furniture for a little while, Belle. The boys've got a lot of crates to open.' He swung his gaze towards Clint. 'Make it some time about . . . mid-afternoon, Clint? I think Belle ought to be ready to leave by then. Will that give you time enough to do your business?'

'My . . . business?' queried Clint.

'Yes. Belle mentioned you might have some sort of – legal thing to arrange with the sheriff there.'

Clint let it sink in for a moment, then nodded slowly. 'Aw, yeah. Almost forgot. OK, I'll call for Belle around mid-afternoon.' He glanced at the girl. 'You'll be ready?'

A mite flustered, she nodded. 'I – think so.'

'Fine.' Forbes took Belle's elbow and Clint was sure she started to pull away, but a hard look from the rancher brought a forced smile back to her lips. 'Let's leave it at that.'

'I – I'll be waiting for you, Clint.'

'I'll be here. Now, I guess we better let you get

95

ready for your special supper this Spanish cook's preparing.'

'Clint. . . .' She took a step forward but Forbes tightened his grip on her arm.

'We'd better go in, Belle, or Conchita'll start throwing my crockery around the kitchen.' He forced a laugh as he looked at the trio of visitors. 'That hot Spanish blood, I guess.'

'More than likely,' allowed Clint, deadpan.

When they left the ranch, Mitch Camden said: 'By God! She – she was *lyin'*. Every time she opened her mouth. God, I know her well, and she was *lyin'*.'

'She had to, Mitch,' Clint said in a flat voice. 'Couldn't you see she was doing what Forbes'd told her to?'

'Why the hell would she do what he told her to?'

'If he said she better put on an act that she was there voluntarily, or he'd have Hank Purcell shoot one of us from cover. . . .' Clint shrugged. 'She'd act just exactly like she did, wouldn't she?'

'My God!' Mitch Camden said. 'I – I believe you could be right, Clinton. I think I know my sister well enough to be sure of that. She did it to save our lives – or leastways, the life of one of us. No matter how she acted, the fact is, she's Rawley Forbes's prisoner.'

'I'm with you, Mitch,' Clint said grimly. 'Way I see it, the next move's gotta be up to us.'

'Mebbe just me,' the sheriff put in, surprising them both.

'Now, you better stay right outta this, Si,' began

Mitch, his tone raspy. 'It's a damn . . . delicate deal, and you buttin' in might put Belle at risk.'

'You mean she ain't at risk already?' the lawman asked bleakly.

'I mean we need to go . . . careful, and not rush this.'

'What you need to realize, Mitch, is I'm the law in this neck of the woods, and there are two or three legal angles involved here. You wait up, now. You've had plenty to say, now it's my turn.'

Clint raised his eyebrows at Si's tone and Mitch was startled too; he opened his mouth to speak, but the sheriff went on:

'The big thing here is, Rawley Forbes is a murderer and Clint is the witness who saw him commit the deed! Right! He's usin' Belle to hold us at bay and I savvy how you two fellers must feel. But I care about Belle's safety as much as you do, and I'm first committed to my oath of office. That means administering the law as I see it, in this or any situation where it's needed.'

'All right, Si,' Mitch said shortly. 'You're doin' your job and that's fine. So you handle all the legal stuff and fix the paperwork, but . . . leave the rest to us.'

Si drew himself up an inch or two and, later, Clint said he thought he heard the old fellow's joints creak.

'Mitch, you ain't listenin'. *I am the law*, here and *now*. So I'm in charge, and you prevent me from doin' my duty as I see it – in *any* way – and I'll slap you in jail so fast your head'll spin clear off your

97

shoulders.'

Mitch Camden was shocked, blinked several times. 'Now listen, Si—'

'No, goddammit! You're the one to do the listenin'. You may not think so, but this is one helluva problem I've got on my hands. An' you might think that I'm too damn old to handle it. Well, I've got news for you, mister: I'm still wearin' my sheriff's star and they'll only take it off me when I'm dead. Or when *I* choose to hand it in. You got that clear in your fool head?'

'Hey! Hey, ease up, Si! I never meant to upset things like this.'

'Then just be quiet and let me think about what we can do to save Belle and stop Clint here from perjurin' himself.'

Mitch was red-faced and mighty uncomfortable as he looked at Clint, who merely gave a slight shrug of his shoulders. But his return look said plainly: *I warned you not to underestimate Si, just because he's old. . . .*

'Well, what . . . what do you want to do, Si?' Mitch asked with quiet exasperation.

The sheriff tilted his head a little and nodded towards the closest, brush-clad hills.

'Seen two flashes there in the last few seconds: sun on rifle barrels, I reckon. You ask me, Rawley's got mebbe a man or two watchin' us. If we look as if we're goin' back to the Forbes ranch, instead of headin' for town I reckon we wouldn't make it. Now don't be stupid and hitch around to look. Let 'em

98

think we ain't seen 'em.'

'Judas, Si! I think I've had a bellyful of this.'

'Then cut out and head for home; Clint an' me'll handle things. But my way. That's how it's gonna be, Mitch. That's how.'

Mitch looked fit to bust but fought down the urge to retort angrily. 'You really think Forbes'd risk havin' Hank or someone shoot us from ambush? I mean: *really*?'

'Man's desperate, or he wouldn't be tryin' to pull off anything like this. His life's at stake here.'

'And Belle's,' Clint dropped in.

'Yep, Belle's too, and yours for that matter, Clint. But Forbes is only thinkin' about Forbes and to hell with anything else.'

'All *right*! But my question still stands: what the hell're you planning to do about it?'

Si McLaren scratched at his wrinkly neck. 'We-ell, Mitch, if Clint here changes his story, has a "loss of memory" like Forbes wants, I'll arrest him for wastin' the law's time, makin' false claims as to what he saw and—'

'Thanks a lot, Si,' Clint said, angrily. 'You put me on the spot very nicely.'

McLaren shrugged his old shoulders and winced as his rheumatics gave a protesting twitch. 'That'd be my duty, Clint. Sorry, but that's it.'

'You're a hard old sonuver, ain't you?'

'Long time since anyone's told me that, but – yeah, I can be when I have to be – or want to be.'

Mitch made an *I give up!* gesture with his arms as

he glanced at Clint. 'Where do we go from here?' he asked.

'Into that line of boulders,' McLaren said instantly. 'They're big enough to give us cover and they penetrate the treeline far enough for us to disappear temporarily. Come on.'

They urged their horses on, Clint and Mitch, both a mite surprised, following the sheriff. He had barely gone into the treeline, now shading the westering sun, when he dismounted and stumbled, but holding his rifle, which he'd snatched from his saddle scabbard. The lawman irritably waved on the other men, clambered between two rocks and settled his body against the contours of one, his rifle coming up to his shoulder.

Clint and Mitch barely had time to register surprise before the Winchester cracked, twice: two very fast shots.

There was a wild yell upslope and a horse staggered out of cover, legs folding, as its rider was thrown over its head. He hit the slope hard and skidded and rolled down towards them, catching up in a low bush.

The sheriff kept the smoking rifle trained on the dazed man and said:

'Well, don't just stand there. Go out and drag that son of a bitch down here. I want to talk to him.'

'Judas! The way he fell – he's – likely dead!' said Mitch Camden.

Si shook his head. 'I shot his hoss, not him. Just go drag him in here before I change my mind and shoot him anyway.'

Clint was already moving to do just that, smiling thinly.

'Si, I don't reckon the folks in Laramie'll *let* you retire.'

CHAPTER 9

CLOSING IN

The man was dazed from his fall off the horse that the sheriff had shot from under him. Clint didn't know him but Mitch Camden did and so did Si McLaren.

He was a roughneck cowboy in looks, but his holster base was tied down and there was a throwing knife in a sheath under his left arm, concealed by the dusty vest he wore. There was a gravel graze above his right eye that started to bleed. He reached under his vest and shouted in pain as Si McLaren cracked his rifle barrel across his wrist.

'Judas Priest! I – I just want a kerchief.'

'Do it slow,' ordered the lawman, jacking a fresh cartridge into the rifle's chamber.

The man's hand was shaking now and he was looking mighty warily at McLaren as he dabbed at the graze with a grimy kerchief.

'How come you're actin' so damn mean, Si?'

'Oh? Actin' mean, am I? Funny, thought it was *you*, hidin' in the brush, ready to backshoot one or all of us, who's the mean one. You got an answer to that, Dobie?'

Dobie licked his lips. 'I – wasn't.'

'Don't lie to me, Dobie. I ain't in a good mood today.'

The rifle barrel cracked on to the man's hands, one of which already had a bruised wrist. Dobie yelled.

'Easy! Hell almighty!' He looked at the silent Mitch Camden and Clint. 'What'd I do?'

Mitch lifted a finger and moved it from side to side.

'Wrong attitude, Dobie. Sheriff's the meanest I've ever seen him today. You see them thunderheads buildin' over Buckshot Ridge? Grey, with lotsa black edgin'. You been here long enough to know what that means?'

'Er . . . could be a whirlie workin' up. . . .'

'Uh-huh. You know what they're like: lots of rain, winds that'll lift the fillings outta your teeth. Well, our sheriff is feeling twice as mean as one of them. So, was I you, I wouldn't risk no gunwhippin' by lyin'.'

'I – ain't . . . *hey*!'

He yelled as the lawman knocked him to his knees with the rifle butt, then placed the muzzle alongside his right ear. 'One shot and you're deaf. And the next one'll cripple you.' The gun barrel moved down

103

to rest just under Dobie's left kneecap. 'You'll never walk again, Dobie.'

Dobie drew the leg away hurriedly, toppled sideways and lay there, terror plain on his face now as he lifted his hands.

'All right. Rawley told me to shoot . . . him.' He gestured to Clint. 'Wound him, but make it plain the next one could kill him if he tried to take the girl . . . an' din' change his story. That's God's truth, I swear!'

'Funny, Dobie,' Si McLaren said, lifting the boot he had placed across the wounded man's neck. 'I think I believe you. Now how's that for a shock to anyone's system?'

Dobie cringed uncertainly.

'I – I was just doin' what I was told.'

'Relax,' growled the lawman. 'Too bad I put you afoot, Dobie. But you can walk OK – at the moment – so why don't you just tell me how things are at Rawley's place, and where the gal is and so on. Then you head over that there mountain and you ever show your face back here in my county. . . .' He paused and gave an on-off smile. 'You got enough imagination to figure out the rest?'

Dobie nodded vigorously.

'Well, then. What're you waitin' for? Start talkin'.'

McLaren winked at Clint and Mitch, who were watching with kind of stunned looks on their faces.

Then Dobie began to talk, so fast the words tumbled over one another, until Si McLaren moved the rifle barrel up close to his ear again.

'Slow an' easy, but clear, Dobie. *Clear*.'

Dobie sat down heavily while he told them the rest, because his legs were too weak to hold him upright.

It was simple enough: just as Clint had figured.

Hank Purcell had 'escorted' Belle back to Forbes, who laid it out plain as day: *do what she was told – exactly.*

Or Clint Reid would be shot dead on the spot, and anyone else who was with him. Dobie didn't know if that included Sheriff Si McLaren, but, if he was there. . . .

'Forbes must be mighty desperate,' opined Clint.

Dobie nodded, wiping some slight discharge from his nostrils across the back of his hairy wrist.

'He – he's – damned scared you're gonna prove you saw him kill that feller. *Mighty* scared. He knows it's a hangin' deal and, well, Rawley's old man was lynched, so it goes.'

Si nodded. 'Before my time, but I recall. It was in Laramie itself. The scum had raped – *raped*, mind you – a young schoolgirl, nine or ten, I think they said. Lynch party weren't too careful how they tied the noose; just castrated Forbes and let him dangle. Died mighty horribly, I hear, and the story is, Rawley seen it all. So, you wanna scare that son of a bitch, just show him a rope noose.'

There was a short period of silence, the faces of the men all looking kind of stiff.

Dobie was almost crying now. 'Can – can I go now?' he stammered, looking appealingly at Si McLaren.

'Not yet,' snapped Clint, looking coldly at the thoroughly scared Dobie. 'What about Belle? Is she OK? How's he treating her?'

Dobie looked worried, but said, haltingly: 'She – she's OK. Leastways last time I saw – I – I got a notion Rawley's kinda – partial to her. Kinda – gone soft on her. Don't think he'll hurt her.'

Clint's hand dropped to his gun butt seemingly of its own accord, and his lips etched a faint white line across his face. 'Why d'you say that?' he asked slowly.

Dobie licked his lips, looking as if he was sorry he had opened his mouth, watching Clint warily.

'Aw, I dunno. Just . . . well, he does little things for her a man does for a woman he . . . admires.'

'Like what?' prompted Clint, tone gritty.

'Er . . . opens a door for her, tells someone to hold her chair for her to settle her at the grub table. An' it's laid with doilies an, stuff. He talks real nice around her, too; cuffed Benny Hooper for cussin' in front of her.'

'Don't sound like Rawley Forbes,' opined Si McLaren.

Mitch frowned, gave a very slight shake of his head, seeing Clint's face. 'Forbes acts the way it suits him at the moment,' he said, flatly, and smiled faintly as he saw agreement in Clint's eyes.

Reid had had a scare, no doubt about that, though he would know, deep down, no matter how Rawley Forbes behaved, it would cut no ice with Belle.

'I . . . I'm just sayin' what I saw,' Dobie added. 'I

106

could be wrong. But can I go now?'

'Sure, Dobie. *Whoa*! Not that door. You can "go" –
straight to my jail, you backshootin' son of a bitch!'

'I – I never—'

'Never quite got around to it, you mean. But you
would've likely bushwhacked the lot of us. Anyway,
don't want you talkin' to Forbes about this meetin'.'

'Damn you, Si!' Dobie almost screamed the words
and abruptly lunged at the old sheriff.

The others were stunned when Si McLaren's Colt
lifted, rammed into Dobie's chest – and fired. Dobie
was thrown backwards. He collapsed, then sprawled
awkwardly, unmoving.

'Arrrh! *Goddamn*!' snapped Si, lifting his right
hand, the gun now back in its holster. His fingers
were clawed. 'Lousy arthritis! Din' mean to kill ol'
Dobe. But you play with the big boys, you gotta be
willin' to risk a *big* accident, I guess. Lost our witness
agin Rawley Forbes, too. *Hell*!'

Clint and Mitch exchanged a quick look. Old Si
was just full of surprises. But there were a couple
more to come.

'Si,' Clint said slowly. 'One thing we've overlooked
– *I* have, anyways. . . .' The sheriff had a small quizzi-
cal frown on his face now. 'Just who *was* the feller
Forbes shot?'

'You mean Roy Denby?'

Clint blinked in surprise. 'You never mentioned
you *knew* him!'

'Didn't. But I sent off a few telegrams to law agen-
cies, askin' if they had anyone on their books

107

reported missin' up this way over the last week or so.' He shrugged. 'One came back, said, an undercover marshal by the name of Russell Draper was on assignment in this neck of the woods, trying to find out who'd been supplying guns to the Indians. To be precise, the bunch that derailed that goods train down Angel Slope way.

'Seems they made a mistake; they were *tryin'* to derail the passenger train – after squaws and money – but got the times mixed up.'

'*R*ussell *D*raper and *R*oy *D*enby: same initials?'

'Yep. Whatever he called himself, he never reported in and they've put him on the missin' list.'

'OK. Sounds reasonable that he's Denby, the one Forbes shot. But it don't really give us much, I guess.'

'Gives us an identity. Description was a bit rough, but more or less fits the feller you saw.'

'Aw, I had him in sight for a few minutes before Forbes came after him and finished him off.'

'Good. You can swear to that at Rawley's trial.'

Clint glanced at him sharply. 'Kinda gettin' ahead of things, ain't you?'

'Well, it's one of the next steps to take, after we tie Forbes to the dead body.'

'Not gonna be easy, way things are.'

'It'll happen sometime.'

' "Sometime" ain't good enough, Si. Dammit, man! Forbes still has Belle.'

Si McLaren nodded slowly. 'Yeah. That *is* a problem. But he can't keep her too much longer by threatenin' to kill you. Not if you do what he wants.'

Clint stiffened. 'What? Withdraw what I said I saw?' Clint snorted. 'You ain't goin' along with that, now. You pratically said you'd kill me yourself if I backed out of makin' the accusation in court. I'll do it though, if I have to, and you or anyone else won't stop me.'

There was a challenge in his tone and in the look he threw the lawman.

Si looked uncomfortable. 'Look, Clint. I don't like playin' with peoples' lives, 'specially innocents, like Belle, caught up in somethin' they can't help.' He produced a wrinkled piece of paper with writing on it. 'Note from Beech Nuttall – he runs the Bijou Hotel in South Laramie. Feller registered under the name of David Roper – those same damn initials again, only back to front – paid up his rent for three days, said he wouldn't be away any longer, had some business to tend to and wanted the room held for him. That was almost a week ago, and Beech is wonderin' if he should sell off the feller's gear or wait a little longer. Not that he'd need the money, mind.'

'Don't sound like the kinda place I'd like.'

'Beech is sorta . . . hungry. Anyway, he asked me to keep an eye out for this "Roper".' He waved the paper briefly. 'Describes him here – and it pretty much fits the description you gave of the feller you saw Forbes kill. Beech mentions he was wearin' a signet ring, too. Sounds like it could be this missin' marshal. Agree?'

'Reckon so,' said Mitch cautiously. 'But we don't have a body to check.'

109

Clint frowned when the sly old lawman smiled crookedly and winked. 'Might have. All that rain we had last night? Muddied up the place to hell an' gone, as usual.'

Clint seemed unsure of the reference, and frowned.

'We get storms like that this time of year,' Mitch explained when he saw Clint's puzzlement. 'You'll get used to 'em after you've been here a little longer. They cause a deal of flooding in the lowlands. Don't usually affect where you've got your land, though, Clint, but they often flood my river pasture.'

'It was one of them 'tween-seasons storms, Clint. We call 'em "Wyoming whirlies". Way the hills are, and how Buckshot Ridge lies, kind of athwart 'em, makes the winds swirl like a kid's spinnin' top.' Si leaned forward as he added, 'An' this one washed away part of that cave-in, which is still loose and ain't had time to pack hard: just enough to expose part of a man's body. Well, what *had* been a man originally, but, accordin' to Heath Early, the ranny who found him, it's kinda mashed outta shape after all that dirt and stones lyin' on top of it. But one arm is almost untouched, and there's a signet ring on the hand. Matches the one old Beech described in his note: a snarlin' wildcat's head with yaller gemstones for eyes.'

Mitch Camden stared a moment in silence, then blew out his cheeks. ' "The best-laid plans of mice and men, eh?" ' For once that whirlie might've done some good, instead of just turning the place into a swamp like they usually do.'

'Reckon Forbes wouldn't agree with you, Mitch. It could put another nail in his coffin.' Then Si tightened his mouth, adding: 'But that lid ain't screwed down yet, by a long shot.'

'It's well under way, though,' said Clint, a slight query in his tone as he looked from one to the other. 'Isn't it?'

Si McLaren gave that thin smile again. 'Providin' we can prove Forbes did bury the body there, by collapsin' that cliff on him, after puttin' three bullets into him, which might be hard to locate, goin' on Heath's description of what he found.'

'Aw, no! We ain't gonna get this close and *still* not nail Forbes?' Clint felt kind of queasy at the thought.

'It's good enough for me, son. But a court of law might look at it a bit different. Want a helluva lot more proof, which *I* can't see is forthcomin' right now.'

'Goddammit to hell!' was Clint's only bitter comment aloud.

But, he thought: *To hell with the law! Let someone else worry about what's legal and what isn't.* All he wanted to do (and urgently) was to get Belle out of Rawley Forbes's clutches.

Any damn way at all!

111

CHAPTER 10

LAST LAUGH

It was imperative that Belle be rescued from Rawley Forbes's ranch.

This was the general concensus of opinion. But there were arguments back and forth as they tried to get a clearer picture of Belle's situation.

Obviously, she had been abducted by Hank Purcell, although Forbes would no doubt come up with another name for it.

An invitation, perhaps, to stay at Forbes's ranch while he unpacked the antique furniture for her interest and inspection – with a possible decision to buy? Eyewash!

'It's the thinnest of covers,' said Mitch irritably. 'Oh, I reckon she's interested in that kind of thing, all right, but Forbes must've leaned on her some to make her exaggerate her enthusiasm for our benefit—'

'Don't agree, Mitch,' cut in Clint Reid, seeing Mitch's deep frown. 'I think that was Belle's way of telling us she was being *forced* to put on that kind of an act. Both you and me knew she had a mild interest in such furniture, but that – was – it. *Mild.* By overemphasizing it she knew we'd start to wonder and get suspicious – if we were smart enough.'

Mitch held up a hand, nodding now. 'Yeah, yeah. You're right! She's plenty savvy enough to come up with something like that, and I reckon she knows we'd be able to figure it out. So, settle for that, and let's work out our next move.' He smiled crookedly. 'Which is. . . ? Hmm. Not forthcoming, gents? Well, me neither. Dammit!'

'Simple,' said Si McLaren, face all red from a coughing, hawking fit, and his one word got their attention promptly. 'We return our dead man, good old Dobie, to Mr Rawley Forbes. While there, I'll tell him I've come to escort Belle back to Mitch's ranch.'

'Hell!' growled Mitch Camden. 'He'll just make excuses for her to stay, and she'll have to go along with him, in case he's got someone sightin'-in on Clint.'

'Not necessarily,' Clint said, a spark of excitment in his tone now. 'Si'll carry a lot more weight than you or me, Mitch, for a start.'

'Yeah, but Forbes'll still use whatever he's got to hold her there. And I think we all agree it's something like: *Do what I say – or Clint – or your brother – will be shot.* Not necessarily killed but "shot" 's enough.'

Si held up a wrinkled hand before Clint could reply. 'Yeah, that's very possible. But s'pose I was to arrest Belle?'

They both stared in surprise.

'*Arrest* her?' echoed Clint. 'What the hell could you arrest Belle for? Lookin' too beautiful? Makin' too many winter clothes for the orphan kids in Laramie?'

Old Si just kept shaking his head slowly. Then he tapped the breast pocket of his worn old jacket with the faded stripes. 'Got me a warrant here for the arrest of one May-Ellen Briscoe, care of the Blue Dove saloon over in Wishbone Bend. Yeah, yeah, she's a saloon gal. A visitin' rancher of some note has accused her of picking his pockets while "entertainin'" him and stealin' forty-three dollars. I can wave that under Rawley's nose, not lettin' him see the name, of course, but give him a flash of the legal seal, and then he's got me to argue with. And I'm here to tell you: no matter what he says he won't win no such argument with me.'

'Unless he demands to see the warrant in full,' Mitch said carefully.

'He'll see as much as I want him to see,' Si snapped confidently. 'And no more. But I guarantee when we leave Forbes's ranch, Belle will be ridin' with us.'

Mitch and Clint exchanged glances. Both started to smile slowly, and Mitch said:

'What the hell're we waiting for?'

It stood a chance of working, Clint reckoned, but no more than that. *Just a chance.*

He knew Forbes well enough to figure the man would balk like a rodeo bull dodging a cowboy trying to throw a saddle on him. But old Si could be surprisingly stubborn when he wanted, and – well, it was going to be an interesting confrontation, all right. Clint was ready to use his six-gun if necessary to get Belle free.

He was right. When they confronted Forbes on his ranch-house porch in the late afternoon, Belle herself standing back in the shadows with Hank Purcell hovering a few feet away, the rancher looked bleakly at the old sheriff.

His contempt for Si was clear in his face and voice.

'Never heard anythin' so stupid. What in hell could you arrest her for?' Forbes snapped, bristling,

'You don't need to know all the whys and wherefores, Rawley,' the sheriff told him firmly, waving the warrant, folded, but with the seal and signature showing. 'All you gotta see – that's *see*, not *touch* – is this official seal of Chief Judge William K. Carmody himself, in Cheyenne. Right here under my finger.' He tapped the paper gently. 'See?'

Forbes reached quickly for it and Si withdrew it just as quickly. 'Look only, dammit! And, you, Belle, I'll save you a mite of embarrassment by not spellin' out exactly why the warrant's been taken out agin you. Just get your things and we'll be on our way. I promise you won't be in too much trouble, but a Carmody warrant has to be served or he'll roast my . . . er . . . well, he'll cuss the hide off of me, at least.'

'I'll just go get my things,' Belle said, unable to keep from smiling now. She turned away on the porch to the nearest door, which a reluctant Hank Purcell held open for her, his eyes narrowed, mouth grim as he glanced at Forbes.

The rancher's face was clouded like one of the worst Wyoming whirlies that had ever threatened this neck of the woods. He raked his murderous eyes around the small group.

'I – still – want – to see – that – warrant,' he gritted, eyes blazing at the old lawman. Hank tensed.

Si McLaren patted the pocket where he had placed the warrant. 'Nothin' to do with you, Rawley. It's Belle who's named in that legal paper. Clint, you – er – wanna go help Belle pack?' He jerked a hand towards the door through which Belle had disappeared with Hank Purcell, but Clint was already striding down the porch towards it. He went to it in a hurry.

Rawley Forbes had somehow managed to get close and he deliberately stepped in front of Clint, colliding with the man, grasping at him for balance, staggering out on to the porch again.

'Hold it!' the older rancher growled.

'Get the hell outta my way, Forbes!' gritted Clint Reid, jostling him roughly.

'Goddammit! This is my ranch. Who the hell you think you are?'

That was as far as Forbes got. Clint punched him in the midriff and the man gagged, grasped the door-jamb, fumbling as his legs bent. He was in the perfect position for Clint to crack an uppercut under his jaw – which he did. It sent Rawley Forbes sprawling on the porch. Even though dazed, Forbes fumbled out his Colt, but Clint kicked it from his hand, then stomped, spreading the hand against the porch's rough-hewn floorboards under his boot heel.

'Mitch,' Clint said, his curt tone bringing Belle's brother's head up fast: 'Go check.'

Mitch was already moving; he shouldered past Clint and the dazed Forbes as the rancher shook his head and started to roll on to hands and knees, preparatory to thrusting to his feet. He swayed, shaking his head to clear it, murder in his eye as he caressed his throbbing hand.

'You're a dead man, Reid.'

'Careful what you say, Forbes. The sheriff's here as a witness to you making threats.'

'The hell with him,' growled Forbes, dabbing at a bleeding mouth where he had hit it when he fell.

Mitch was moving through the door when he sud-denly felt an iron claw grip his shoulder, spin him around and send him staggering across the porch. Before he straightened up he saw Si McLaren disap-pearing through the doorway in his place, the sheriff calling over his shoulder:

'Stay outta it, Mitch. This is official law business.'

'Get after him, Clint!' Mitch yelled as he stumbled.

Clint was already going through the doorway into

the gloom of the ranch house, calling: 'Belle! Belle!'

'H-here – Clint. I . . . oh!' Her voice cut off abruptly as Hank Purcell yelled:

'I've got a gun under her ear, Reid. Stay back.'

'Judas Priest, Hank!' bawled a startled Forbes. 'The hell're you doin'?'

'Right now, I'm about to trade the gal for a clear getaway. Any takers?'

'Drop it, Hank.' They heard Si McLaren's voice and Belle's scream, followed by the sounds of a brief scuffle, then two fast shots, and, a heartbeat later, a third, but this last had a different sound to it, as if the gun had fired with the barrel close to the floor. Then a body slumped and Belle cried shrilly:

'Clint! Mitch! He's shot the sheriff!' The rest was muffled as a hand was clamped across her mouth.

'Stay back, all of you,' shouted Purcell. 'The sheriff's dead. You wanna join him? Well, be my guests!'

'*Christ*, Hank!' bellowed Rawley Forbes, buying in at last. You've done it now, you blamed fool! You can't kill a lawman and—'

'What the hell! You turnin' on me, too, Rawley?'

'Got no choice, Hank. Not if you've really killed old Si. Nothin' I can do to help you now!'

'Damn you, Rawl! I done it for you. Like everythin' else since you saved my life in the War. I've stuck my neck out so far, and so often, I feel like a goddamn turkey at Thanksgivin'!'

'Better let the girl go, Hank,' Forbes advised. 'You'll only make it worse for yourself if you don't'

'And that's the truth,' Clint called, crouching by another doorway that led into the yard behind Forbes's house. It was heading towards sundown now and long shadows made dark patches against the glowing light of the setting sun. 'Let Belle go, Hank. She just got caught up in this deal through no fault of her own.'

'And she's gonna get me outta it, too. You try to stop me – *any* of you – and you can start figurin' what you're gonna put on her headstone.'

'For God's sake, man!' roared Mitch Camden suddenly. 'This is no fault of hers. Let her go.'

'Ah, Camden. Yeah, well, I've got plenty to square with you, you uppity bastard! You always treated me like dirt and—'

'Because you *are* dirt, Hank.'

'Judas, Mitch!' snapped Clint. 'For Chrissakes don't rile him any more! He's likely to harm Belle.'

'Hey, Reid! I heard that. An' you're absolutely right. I will *harm* her, if you don't pull back an' let me get a couple hosses. Fact, why don't you go get 'em for me? But if I find my cinchstrap's loose, or somethin', well, use your imagination, you son of a bitch!'

'All right, Hank, all right! I'll saddle you a damn horse.'

'You'll saddle two,' yelled Purcell. 'I'm warnin' you, Reid. Try any of your tricks, and, if I have to, I'll ride double outta here with the gal sittin' in my lap. An', nice as that may be, you got my word it'll take you one helluva time to find where I eventually dump her. *And* you won't like what you do find.'

119

'Take it easy,' Clint said as calmly as he could, his mouth dry. He turned to Forbes. 'Any chance of sneaking up on him while I get the horses?' he asked in a low voice.

Forbes smiled crookedly. 'Corral's out in the open. See? Just past that line of tree. I'd do what Hank wants. He can be mighty mean, and the girl makes a good hostage.'

Clint swore. 'You oughta know, you son of a bitch! I'm not finished with you yet, either.' He shoved the rancher aside roughly, as he called to Hank Purcell that he was making his way to the corral. 'And let me hear Belle. So I know she's all right.'

He held his breath while he waited through an interminable silence that, in reality, was no longer than five or six seconds.

'Clint?' Her voice was strained but that was to be expected, he thought, as his heart started thumping against his ribs. 'I – I'm all right. Please don't take any risks. I – I'll go with Hank and do whatever he wants until he's clear, and and wait for you to come.'

God almighty! Clint thought. *Surely she doesn't really believe he's going to let her go?*

Aloud, he called: 'I hear you, Belle. Just do like he says, and you'll be all right. That right, Hank? Or you want some other kinda deal?'

The laughter that came through the dusk was mocking; it drifted away as Hank Purcell said:

'You are somethin', Reid. Not sure what. But you sure are somethin'. I'm almost sorry to leave you, but. . . . Hurry up and get them broncs saddled before it gets any darker. *Come on*! *Move*! I got places to go.'

Clint's hands closed into fists down at his sides as he stood on the rise and watched Hank Purcell ride out with Belle on the mounts he had saddled.

She sat stiffly in her own saddle as Hank manoeuvred his sorrel constantly, keeping her between him and Rawley Forbes.

'Good man, Hank,' Forbes said with a sour look at Clint Reid. 'Dependin' on your point of view, of course.'

'He'll be good and dead when I catch up with him, specially if he harms Belle.'

'We-ell – no tellin' with Hank Purcell. He's his own man and plenty of times you just dunno which way he's gonna jump.'

'He'll jump straight into Boot Hill if he hurts – or even tries to hurt her.'

Forbes smiled crookedly. 'You don't think Hank's scared of you, do you?'

'No. But he ought to be at least *leery* of me – if he has any brains.'

'Oh, he's smart enough, is Hank. I mean, look at you, now. What else can you do except stand here and watch him ride out with your gal?'

Forbes gave a little start that wiped the leer off his face when he looked into Clint's deadly eyes.

'I'll catch up with him,' Clint said quietly. 'And you and me've got a heap to settle yet. Whatever happens, I'll be back for you, Forbes.'

'Huh!' The grunt was all the rancher could manage and Clint saw he was angry with himself when his tongue automatically ran around his dry lips. He cleared his throat but Clint was already hurrying up the slope where he could see part of a man's body: an arm in an old jacket with faded stripes in the cloth.

Si McLaren. . . .

To Clint's surprise, he found the battered old sheriff still alive: at least he was breathing slowly, raggedly and laboured, eyes half-open and finding it hard to focus.

As he knelt beside the lawman, Forbes came up and thumbed back his hat.

'Well, I'll be! Knew old Si was tough, but – hell! Looks like Hank got him twice – in the chest.'

'Hand me that saddle canteen,' Clint snapped, loosening his collar, taking off his hat and using it for a pillow for Si to rest his head on.

'Take it easy, old-timer. Hurry up with that water, Forbes.'

'It won't help. He's too old, too far gone—'

Forbes jumped as Clint's gun appeared in his hand, the hammer back under his thumb. '*Hurry it up*, I said!'

'Judas! You *are* fast, ain't you?' He lifted a hand quickly as the gun barrel pointed at him. 'OK, *OK*!'

He knelt by Si's head as Clint held it up so water could trickle past the old wrinkled lips.

'Just a little, Si. No! Not too much. Just let it moisten your mouth. Uh-huh. That better?'

Si McLaren's pain-filled eyes sought Clint's face

and he nodded once.

'Not – not gonna make – it, you – know. . . .'

'Who says?' Clint asked, with a faint smile. 'You ain't a doctor. You never can tell.'

'I – can.' One heavily veined hand crawled up across the bloody cloth of his shirt, fumbled and picked at his badge, trying to free it from the cloth.

'What're you doing, Si?'

Those old eyes rolled in Clint's direction. His mouth worked a few times before he rasped weakly – 'Y-you. . . .'

'What?' Clint frowned. 'Me? What, Si?'

'You – yours. . . .'

'Come on. Don't worry about it. I'll look after the badge for you till you get better, if that's what you want.'

'No! Nah. . . .' Si rolled his head from side to side, once each way, face very grey now. He let go of the badge, groped for Clint's hand and guided it to the metal star. He struggled and croaked: 'C-Clint Reid. I – I name you – Deputy Sheriff – of – Lar-a-mie – County.'

'The hell!' said Rawley Forbes.

Clint was too surprised to say anything for a few seconds, then:

'You – you better rest, Si. It won't do you no good to—'

'S-s-say you – acc-accept.' McLaren made an effort to struggle to a sitting position but it was too much. As he sank back he slid his gaze to the stunned-looking Forbes. 'Y-you're – a – witness – Rawley. . . .'

123

'Hey! Wait up, Si. I – aw, this is loco!'

'N-no!' Si's head rolled sideways again. 'C-Clint only needs to say – "yes". . . .'

Clint's gaze locked with the oldster's, saw the pleading there and almost without being conscious of what he was doing, nodded, saying: 'OK, Si. I accept the badge of office.'

'G – Good. Now – y-you watch your – s-sorry ass, Raw-Rawley. Not-not just 'cause of Clint. . . .' He paused, his thin old chest heaving as he laboured for enough breath to finish what he wanted to say. Grim-faced, Clint rested a hand on the wrinkled forehead, fingers caressing lightly.

'It's OK, Si. I'll – accept the badge.'

The dying lawman nodded, looking straight up into Clint's face.

'Rawley,' he croaked, and the rancher frowned, leaned closer. 'Wa – watch – Hank . . . with that – gal.'

'*Hank*?' echoed Forbes in surprise.

Si made a series of grunting sounds and Forbes glanced at Clint, who shrugged lightly, indicating he didn't know what Si was trying to say.

Then the sheriff told them, in a series of rasping syllables.

'Hank hates – that – g-gal. Could – kill her.'

'Hank hates most folk,' Forbes said with a crooked smile. 'He won't harm her unless I tell him to.'

'No!' Si rasped. 'He – really hates her – 'cause you – you're – inn-erested in her. He's – jealous.'

Then Si sagged abruptly and his eyes closed.

Clint thought the sound he made must be the

death rattle, but, later, thinking about it, he decided it had been a laugh! Si McLaren's very last laugh. . . .

There was some irony in the situation, he allowed: a man like Rawley Forbes, bully, murderer, gun-runner – and worse – being forced by circumstances beyond his control to witness the deputization of a man who was not only his sworn enemy, but now, an official lawman besides.

And one who could arrest him whenever he felt he had the necessary evidence. As Clint pinned the sur-prisingly heavy badge to his shirt he said:

'I think Si was right, Forbes. You'd better start watching your sorry ass!'

Forbes snorted, scowling. 'This ain't legal.'

Clint smiled crookedly: he wasn't sure one way or the other, but suddenly his Colt's barrel was pressing up beneath the startled Forbes's jaw.

'I've taken the job, and I'm making it legal.'

Rawley Forbes's head was pressed to one side by the pressure of the gun. His eyes stared uncertainly at Clint, seeing no friendliness in the young rancher's face.

'I've got no time to try to convince you I'm legally a deputy lawman now, so you better tell me, and quickly: where's Hank taking Belle?'

Forbes stiffened, then the beginnings of a crooked smile showed as he shook his head once. 'No idea.'

Clint didn't move immediately, or even ease up on the pressure. He simply looked bleakly into the rancher's eyes, let the impact work for no more than a few seconds, then moved his Colt so fast it was only a blur of movement.

Rawley Forbes staggered sideways, hat spinning off, falling to his hands and knees, his face bleeding and bruised in several places. Dazed and in agony, he suddenly felt Clint's Colt's barrel pressing into the back of his neck.

'Not sure whether you didn't hear my question or I didn't hear your answer. So I'll give you a second chance: where – did – Hank – take – Belle?'

'Hey! Easy there, Clint,' murmured Mitch in some alarm but said no more when Clint turned his head a little and winked.

'Sorry, Mitch. Think mebbe the power of being a real deputy has gone to my head. Can't seem to help myself. Got this urge to push people around, you know?'

Forbes's face was contorted now, bleeding from above one ear, his nose, and a cut on his left cheek. His breath whistled through his nostrils as he looked up at Reid towering over him, his pistol cocked.

Forbes swallowed audibly.

'Listen! I – I *really* dunno. Wait. Judas Priest! I – I mean it. When we first decided to use the gal, Hank told me he had a – a "hidey-hole" he called it, some-where up in the Buckshots. Used it when he an' a coupla other fellers went on a week-long caper one time an' tried their hands at rustlin', even a stage-coach hold-up. I – I never knew exactly where, but I think it's somewhere on the ridge. He mentioned the west side once. That's all I know. I swear!'

Clint gave him a hard, cold look.

'Well, you just tag along and show me, and we'll see how good you recollect.'

'Look. Hank's kinda – well, he's still got a piece of shrapnel somewhere in his head. Got it at that big fight at Flintlock Crossin' near the end of the War. We got blown outta a shell-hole we'd stumbled into and I caught some shrapnel in the back, but Hank got it in the head, and we found a wanderin' hoss an' we rode double, Hank hangin' over the saddle and me tryin' not to slide off the rump.

'Another blast killed the hoss and I dragged Hank into a nearby camp. Turned out to be Rebs but their doctors patched us up. They couldn't get the shrapnel outta Hank's head: too close to his brain, they reckoned. Said he'd haveta be careful, an' not get too riled-up or drink too much – aaah! They din' really know what might happen. They were shovin' wounded through almost head to toe, an' the War was almost over, anyway. They just turned us loose.'

'Never mind the story. You find this "hidey-hole". You've got till sun up. If you haven't located it by then, it'll be the last sunrise you ever see. Savvy?'

Forbes's eyes narrowed dangerously and he nodded his head slowly, mopping at his face with a crumpled kerchief. Clint knew the man was ready to explode.

'I – savvy,' Forbes grated.

'Then let's go,' Clint said, bringing up his Colt again for emphasis.

'This ain't over yet, Reid.'

'No. Not till one of us is dead, Rawley.'

127

Forbes gave him a crooked smile.
'I'll settle for that.'

CHAPTER 11

BUCKSHOT RIDGE

Clint knew he couldn't trust Forbes as far as he could kick him.

But he had to use the man now and the sooner he found out if he was being led into a trap the better: get it over with, shoot to kill and make damn sure his bullets went where they were meant to.

It wasn't a new situation; he'd been in a few similar ones over the years, not counting the War. There had been rustlers – or intending ones, land-grabbers (a lot of them when this part of the country was opened up for settlement), confidence tricksters and – well, a man had to know how to use a gun, and practise with it regularly if he wanted to survive.

There was no use fooling yourself that the lawlessness was just going to stop. When a new range was opened for settlers they were usually outnumbered by the grifters and plain thieves who were not bothering to put any fancy trimmings on their deeds. Just moving in and taking over, and leaving a string of fresh-dug graves, too easily filled.

He had heard a lot of stories about Rawley Forbes and his roughshod, boot-kicking, gunwhipping methods when he moved in on range that he coveted. If a man was unlucky enough to be there already he either moved out, pronto, of his own accord, or he was carried out.

So Clint came alert when he realized that Forbes had worked his way through the many draws and gulches so as to deliberately confuse him, and started down the east side of Buckshot Ridge.

'You need a compass?' he called to the rancher, who was riding a few yards ahead.

Forbes hipped in the saddle, frowning. 'I ain't lost.'

'Nor me. You said Hank's hideaway was somewhere on the west side; this here looks like the east one to me.'

'Yeah, well, it is. Figured might be better to come up – or rather, *down* – on him from this side. "Claim the high ground" like they used to say in the army.'

'Good notion,' admitted Clint. 'Long as you keep that bronc of yours from sendin' a warning.'

'My bronc?' Forbes's voice echoed his puzzlement.

'Three times I seen you nudge him through loose gravel so it slipped on down the slope, rattlin' all the way. Good as a telegraph, tellin' whoever's below that someone's up above and on the way down.'

'The hell I did! If, and I say *if*, that happened, it was accidental. You think I don't want to get the gal away from Hank when he's in such a loco mood?'

'Well, I think you'd figure you had an advantage if we – that's you an' me – didn't get Belle free.'

'Now why would. . . ?'

'A blind man could see you haven't forgotten I'm the only witness to you killing that marshal. You have Belle, you figure you got a lever to keep me quiet about what I saw.'

'My, my! Don't we get all smart-mouthed 'n' smug, once we get a piece of tin pinned to our shirt!'

Clint smiled thinly. 'That's the way it goes, they tell me. So, just keep ridin', Rawley. but swing over that ridge and angle down the west side.'

Clint backed up his words with his six-gun and he saw Forbes give a start and drop his hand away from his own gun butt.

'Just what I was gonna do, dammit!' Rawley Forbes snapped.

'Then we got no problem.' Clint jerked his gun barrel. 'Let's get it done.'

As they made their way up to the top of the ridge and halted briefly in the trees before starting slowly down to the west side, Clint saw that a small corral had been built of handy rocks and deadfalls and now housed four or five horses. He used his Colt to sign for Forbes to stop, peering through the gathering dusk.

'Uh-huh. Can just make out part of a shingle roof about ten yards to the right of that rock corral. My guess is that's Hank's "hidey-hole", his getaway mount's all nice and handy. Plays it careful, don't he?'

Forbes smiled. 'That shrapnel never did cross-up his thinkin'. Only when he got what he uses for a brain overheated, or pickled in red-eye.'

'And if we'd stuck to the trail you were taking me on first,' Clint said slowly and menacingly, 'I'd never have known that cabin or corral was there – until Hank blew me out of the saddle.'

Forbes shrugged. 'Thought it was worth a try,' he admitted, kind of smugly.

'Uh-huh,' Clint said mildly, then he rammed his spurs into his mount's flanks, leaping it forward.

Rawley Forbes didn't even have time to curse as the horse slammed into his own mount just in front of his leg.

Man and animal went down in a thrashing heap, the falling horse so taken by surprise it only got out the beginning of a starled whinny, before rolling and kicking as it started sliding down the slope. Forbes frantically kicked his boots free of the stirrups and desperately clawed himself out of the way as the horse slid down towards him.

He just managed it, clinging to a stunted brush as the animal slid on its back, whinnying loudly now, and going past him. He tugged at his Colt but found Clint's mount almost standing on top of him now, the man's rifle pointing at his head.

Clint spoke quietly to his own quivering mount as it rolled its eyes, watching Forbes's horse some distance below, scrambling to its feet on a patch of turf.

It was a well-trained range horse and made no attempt to run off, but stood there, snorting a little, pawing the ground with a forefoot, waiting for its master to show approval – or otherwise – of its actions.

Forbes looked as if he wanted to murder every living thing within reach, but got control, grabbed the leery horse's reins and glared up at his captor.

'What you – think that – gained you?' he panted.

'Nothing much, 'cept it likely saved me from a nudge over the rim that would've had me trying to sprout wings; or even a bullet in the back. The shot would bring Hank, of course, but he'd be happy enough to see you, I guess.'

'So? What now?'

'Been thinkin' on that. If I was to shoot you—'

'Hey! Wait up!'

'Just stay still. Yeah, the shot would still bring Hank a-running, all right, but I could pick him off, and – well, then all I'd have to do is go into the cabin and untie Belle and, who knows? We just might live happily ever after.'

'You're loco! Hank'd never fall for that.'

'No. He'd likely get sneaky and come at me from some other trail I don't know about. Might even kill Belle. Either way, you wouldn't live to see it.'

Forbes sobered fast. 'Hold it, will you, *hold it*! OK, so I tried somethin' and it didn't work. You can't blame me for tryin'.'

'But I can blame you for a lot of my other troubles. So you get a chance to make it up to me a little; we

133

walk up to the cabin and you call Hank out and. . . . Can you figure it from there?'

'Reckon so,' Forbes said carefully. 'But you forgot one thing.'

'I get forgetful at times,' Clint admitted wryly. 'Tell me what you're talkin' about.'

'Hank's cunnin'. He wouldn't just come out, even if he recognized my voice. Oh, he'd come eventually – with the gal held in front of him and a knife at her throat, or his gun in her ribs.'

Forbes was starting to grin and Clint felt his belly freeze as Forbes added: 'Just like now, where he's standin' in the doorway down there, with good ol' Belle in front of him. Mmm, not sure if that's a gun or a knife he's holdin'. You make it out?'

Clint swore and slowly held his rifle out to one side as he saw the scene Forbes had just described. He dropped the weapon without being told, just as Belle cried his name.

'Oh, Clint!' There was tremendous relief in her voice. 'I knew you'd come'.'

'Oooooh! I'm all shaky an' breakin' out in a cold sweat,' yelled Hank, acting it up. 'Clint's here!' he cried, falsetto. 'Hoo-goddamn-ray!'

'I am here, Belle,' Clint said quietly, dismounting.

'Yes!' she cried again, emphasizing the short word.

'Don't sound so happy, you bitch!' Hank growled, shaking her. 'Just makes him easier to kill.' Then he began to laugh. 'Might even let you watch. You like that?'

Then Clint Reid took a quick step to his left, Colt

134

coming up in that slick, smooth draw that had earlier given Forbes cause to be mighty leery of the new deputy. Clint pressed his gun muzzle into Forbes's neck, below his ear, his left hand holding the startled man by the back of his trouser belt.

'Know you don't care much for Belle, Hank. But how about good ol' Rawley here? They tell me you got a soft spot for him 'cause he saved your lousy neck one time.'

'You leave him be, you son of a bitch!' Hank almost screamed. 'You think I can't pull this trigger, whether you nail me or not?' He paused, laughed briefly as he twisted his left hand in Belle's hair, bored in the gun barrel, making her cry out in pain. 'You wanna see who's really got the upper hand here?'

Clint wasn't game enough to call his bluff.

Even if his shot killed Hank outright. there would be an instinctive convulsion of his gun hand, or, just the jerk as Clint's bullet slammed him back would likely be enough to trigger the Colt now pressed against Belle's head.

'All right,' he said with resignation, letting his shoulders slump. 'All *right*!'

Hank grinned at his victory and eased up the pressure on the gun . . . a little, anyway.

'See you got some sense after all,' Hank crowed, and Rawley Forbes stiffened.

'Hank, no! Don't! He never gives up that easy. He's got some move that. . . .' Forbes sounded near frantic.

'His next move is droppin' dead,' Hank yelled but, even as he swung his Colt away from the girl, Clint took a quick step to the side, pulling Forbes off balance.

Rawley yelled, stumbled, and was thrust face first into the gravel with Clint's boot pressing into his spine.

'Let's continue this conversation, Hank. But we'll do it my way – unless you want Rawley's brains spattered on your boots.'

He had leaned forward so that his Colt barrel rested against the back of the squirming Forbes's head.

'He's dead, either way, Hank,' Clint told him, making his voice cold and disinterested. He gave Forbes a kick in the side, making him groan. 'Aaah! You're too stupid to deal with. Let's get it over with. Say *adios* to your pard.'

He cocked the hammer hard, making a distinctly audible click.

'*Hank*!' Forbes almost screamed the word. 'Back off! Back *off*.'

'OK, Rawley. The bastard'll keep! We'll square things, you an' me together. Reid? You want her, you come an' get her.'

Hank savagely shook Belle, dragging her off her feet by her hair. She reached up swiftly with both hands, face contorted with the pain. He shook her violently again and bared his teeth at the rigid Clint.

'You comin', you sonuver?'

Belle screamed as he twisted the hair this time,

before shaking her enough to make her fall to her knees.

'All right! Damn you, Hank!'

'Just get away from Rawley.'

'No!' Clint sounded emphatic. 'I don't want Belle harmed, but you hurt her again and I'll blow Forbes's head off, then come after you; it'll take a cavalry troop to stop me. Or mebbe they wouldn't even do it, because you will die no matter what.'

'You're loco! Plumb – damn – loco! *I* got the upper hand here.

'No, Hank. Just trying to make you realize that I'm serious.' He turned and hauled Forbes to his feet, rested the blade foresight at the corner of the man's right eye.

'Convince him, Forbes. Or I'll use you as an object lesson.'

'Christ! Hank's right. You are plumb loco.'

Clint moved the blade sight half an inch and Forbes yelled and squirmed.

'You don't want to wear an eyepatch for the rest of your life. *Tell him!*'

'H-Hank! Back off, man! Back off! Or he'll blind me.'

Hank glared and Clint tensed; he was gambling on the man's near-unhealthy regard for Rawley Forbes. Was it powerful enough for him to comply? Let the girl go in exchange for Forbes's life?

'What'll it be, Hank?' he called. 'You might figure it's a stand-off, but I guess I love Belle enough to take this chance. Because if anything did happen to her, you'd never take more'n two steps before you were on the ground with my bullet in you. And it wouldn't be a killing shot, Hank. You'd live till sundown, with all kinds of pain. See, I lived with Indians nigh on a year – Mescaleros. And, man, they fair turned my stomach the way they treated some of their prisoners. I don't reckon I've forgotten their ways.'

His words seemed to hang in the air and Hank kept alternating his looks between Forbes and the girl.

'He – mean that – Rawl?' Hank's voice had a little break in it when he asked.

'I dunno, Hank. But don't take the chance, feller! There'll be another time.' Forbes looked at Clint, his face kind of grey. 'For you an' me, I mean, Hank.'

'I think you have a death wish, Forbes,' Clint told the rancher curtly. Then he raised his voice. 'Hank! I meant what I said. And I always keep my word. Always! So when I tell you now to ride out and leave Belle right where she is you'd better do just that.' He paused, then added coldly: 'You know the alternative. So make up your mind. Now!'

CHAPTER 12

'KILL 'EM BOTH!'

Clint's last word echoed, drifting away across the edge of the drop, and still Hank hadn't made a move.

Beads of sweat were now standing out on Forbes's forehead and he clenched his fists down at his side.

'Jesus, Hank! Do like he says or—'

'You really are fallin' for her, ain't you, Rawl?'

Forbes frowned, a mite startled the way Hank was thinking. 'Hank, never mind that. You've got it wrong, anyway, an' if you wanta live, *let – her – go*! He's gonna kill you, otherwise. Can't you see that?'

Hank's face showed a brief surprise, then he glared at Clint. 'That right, Reid? You think you'll kill me?'

'You harm her, Hank, you – are – dead. You can bet on that.'

'Uh-huh. But how about I ride out now – an' take

139

her with me?'

'*No!*' roared Forbes. 'No, Hank. Just let her go. Be better all round.'

'You're just sayin' that because you're *fallin'* for her. I see the way you look at her. Should've killed her long ago. Judas, Rawl! You any me don't need *her*. We get along just fine, have done for years, an'—'

'Just forget her, dammit!' Forbes was sweating now, his voice edging almost on panic: he *knew* what Hank was capable of when he got his mind locked into a single, overwhelming thought. 'Reid's gonna kill us both if we don't do like he says, for Chrissake!'

'Good advice, Hank,' Clint said quietly, trying to hide the building tension he felt grabbing at his guts. 'Just drop your gun and ride out. Take Forbes with you if you like, but do it! Or die where you stand.'

Still Hank hesitated, stubborn as a Missouri mule, hating to have to give in.

He looked steadily at the white-faced girl, then at Forbes, and, finally, at Clint Reid.

'You let us both ride out?'

'If *both* means you and Forbes, yeah.' Clint's Colt was steady on Hank now and the man tightened his lips.

Then, suddenly, he jammed his spurs into his mount, snatched the reins of Belle's horse and crouched in his saddle, heading downslope . . . taking them all by surprise.

Belle cried out, swayed and jerked, trying to keep her seat as the horse launched itself in a clumsy lunge.

'*Belle! Jump!*' Clint bawled before the horse found its stride and gathered speed.

It was dangerous, even desperate, advice but it was all Clint could think of at that moment. She hesitated as Hank's efforts dragged the horse towards the steepest edge of the drop-off above the river: twelve, maybe fifteen feet below.

Clint's heart was in his mouth as the distance closed to a couple of yards and he shouted involuntarily:

'No – don't!' meaning his words for Hank. But instead it confused the girl and her pale face showed her bewilderment, even as the horse skidded towards the edge.

Then she made her move. But instead of trying to drag the mount's head around, turning it away from the edge, she jerked the reins and threw her weight to the left. The already disconcerted animal swerved, began to slow, changed its mind, and swung back the other way. *Too mixed up!*

Belle cried out in alarm as she was thrown violently from the saddle, hit the slope, and rolled swiftly towards the drop-off. The horse whinnied shrilly and went over, its weight causing the edge to crumble and start to break away in crooked lines winding rapidly in Belle's direction, as the ground split.

In a moment her cry of alarm, now edged with fear, echoed through Clint's mind like a tolling bell.

She plummeted down with dirt and rocks, the horse already below her, twisting and kicking as it fell.

141

'*Christ*!' yelled Forbes, his face contorted as he swung towards Reid. 'You've killed her, you stupid bastard!'

But Clint had his own problems with his balking mount. He hauled on the reins, legs rigid in the stirrups, instinctively trying to turn away from the drop. But the mount was afraid and confused, lost its footing, skidded with stiffened forelegs, and took its rider with it as it plunged over the cliff, falling after the girl.

On the rim, Forbes succeeded in hauling his mount to a stop. He rose in his stirrups in time to see both the girl and Clint Reid hit the river in twin, mighty splashes, seconds apart.

When the spray settled he saw the girl in the shallows, sprawled awkwardly, obviously unconscious, if not worse. Her horse was limping badly, shaking water from its head and mane, dragging itself around the rocks.

Clint was dazed from the jolt of hitting the water but he had come down in a deeper pool than Belle and, to a certain extent, this had cushioned his fall. Where Belle had landed was nowhere near as deep, and she must have been knocked unconscious by the impact.

He *hoped* that was all, anyway.

Head ringing, body feeling the way it had after an overturned wagon crash he remembered from the War, Clint waded to her, fumbled her awkwardly into his arms and staggered and stumbled his way to the bank.

She jarred hard as he set her down, off balance

142

and arms too weak to do it as gently as he would have liked.

Above, Forbes had stopped his mount and slid his rifle from the saddle scabbard.

But he paused as he levered a cartridge into the breech. He was afraid of hitting the girl; even as Clint lurched into some low rocks with her Reid's legs gave way under him and he dropped to his knees beside Belle, pushing strands of wet hair back from her face.

As Clint crouched over her, the low rocks shielded him from Forbes's view.

Cursing, the older rancher lowered the gun hammer and got to his feet, looking for a safe way down a precarious trail to the river. It was the only way now: get to the damn rocks and blast Clint Reid to hell, then. . . .

'I got 'em, Rawl! I can just see 'em through a gap. Right – about – there.'

Forbes cringed as he saw Hank, a few feet to his left, kneeling now, rifle angled down, tensed to shoot, sighting carefully at the man and woman below, whom he could see and Forbes couldn't.

'Judas, Hank! Don't risk it, pard.'

Hank looked at him bleakly. 'Hell, I can get 'em both and our worries are over! Ten seconds at the most.'

'Goddammit! I want the girl alive. To hell with what *you* think!' Forbes levelled his rifle at the startled Hank's head.

'Hey, Rawl! The hell you doin'? It's *me*, for Chrissake!'

143

'I – know!' Forbes said heavily, rifle held steady.

Hank swallowed as he saw Forbes's face, sighting down the rifle.

'Ah, hell!' Hank suddenly said in disgust. 'He's dragged her deeper into the damn rocks now, anyway, and I can't even see 'em! Judas Priest, Rawl! Neither of us can get a shot now.'

'They won't get far. The girl's horse is hurt and they'll have to ride double on Reid's.' Rawley Forbes pointed to his right. 'Looks like a way down there. Might have to work across pretty slow in one part, but seems to me it'll come out right by them rocks. Let's move!'

He started to stride away and Hank said, 'How the hell we gonna get the hosses down there? They can't tippytoe on a narrow trail like that.'

'We'll have to try. Unless you wanna run 'em off the cliff into the river like Reid did?'

'Aaah! You shoulda let me shoot 'em.'

Looking at the narrow trail, clinging to the cliff face, Forbes silently agreed, but only said quietly, 'You might get another chance.'

Then he stiffened, surprised at the raw hate on Hank's face as the man said:

'I damn well *better*!'

Rawley Forbes swallowed: he'd pushed that crazy Hank about as far as he dared. . . .

He might even have real trouble keeping him from killing the girl.

The hell with Reid: he didn't matter. But Forbes wanted that woman – alive – at any cost.

144

He reined up suddenly, halfway down the dangerous trail, and Hank almost collided with him. His
face went pale as he fought his grey and hauled it
almost up on to its hind legs with his effort. *Of course
Reid mattered!*

'*Goddamn*, Rawl!' Hank bawled, fighting the confused and badly frightened mount as part of the trail
crumbled beneath its stomping hoofs. 'The name of
hell you doin'?'

Forbes had a few more moments of settling his
own mount, and he patted its quivering neck as he
looked back at Hank.

'Sorry, Hank. Had a thought that Reid don't
matter but—'

'Well, he don't! He's just a big goddamn fly
buzzin' around an' botherin' us, and about to get
swatted.'

'No!'

'*No*? What the hell's got into you?'

'He's a *deputy* now, Hank. A *lawman*!'

'Aah, I seen that badge he's wearin'. Makes a good
target, eh?'

'Hell, him wearin' that badge makes all the difference! In this country you don't kill lawmen. Whether
they're new to the job or not. It's just one of them
things.'

Hank frowned, squinting at the rancher. 'The
hell's wrong with you, Rawley? *You're* the only witness
still alive who seen old Si deputize Reid. So who
cares? We kill him, rip the damn badge off his shirt
and throw it away. Who'll know the difference?'

145

Tight-lipped, Forbes said, 'Belle knows he was deputized.'

'Then we kill her, too. We gotta, Rawl! No one'll know then. Hell, in any case old Si never had no chance to register that he'd deputized Reid. Ah! You're worryin' about nothin'. Let's just go and shoot 'em, tie a few rocks to the bodies and drop 'em in a deep part of the river. All our troubles are over then.'

It sounded easy – even practical, Forbes admitted to himself, but. . . .

'You forget Reid's the one seen you kill that marshal? Seen it happen, Rawley. You shoulda shut his mouth with a bullet long ago.'

'I ain't forgot. But. . . .'

Hell! That damn woman had got under his skin, somehow, and it didn't rest easy with him, thinking about her weighted body on the bottom of the river; the fish and whatever else was down there – feeding.

Then again, he knew damn well he'd hate the feel of a hempen noose around his neck. The one enduring fear he had carried with him all the years since he had witnessed his father's lynching.

In the heat of battle, amidst the bayonets and whistling bullets, even the thundering hoofs of a cavalry charge, he had held the thought that if he was going to die, it would be quicker than that sickening, slow strangulation he had watched take his father: unable to even close his eyes or turn his head away. . . .

They reached the foot of the narrow trail and the

rolling-eyed mounts were beginning to settle down again, snorting and sweating. Forbes looked across at Hank, pointed at the clump of rocks where Reid and the girl had last been seen.

'Let's go find 'em,' he gritted.

'Now you're talkin',' Hank yelled, and rammed in his spurs.

CHAPTER 13

THE BADGE

They heard the clatter of hoofs as Forbes and Hank spurred their mounts into the rocks that – at present – hid them.

Clint Reid knew they could expect no mercy from the hunters, and that included the girl, because she knew things now that could be dangerous knowledge as far as Forbes was concerned.

Maybe it was true that Forbes was actually falling for her, but he was ruthless and, while he might be reluctant to harm Belle, he wouldn't hesitate if it meant saving his own skin.

Hank was a different proposition, a more *dangerous* one, because for years he had practically worshipped the ground that Forbes walked on because the man – in Hank's opinion, anyway – had saved his life. Likely it was true enough and it was one of nature's strange whims that someone like Hank, mean, arrogant and a born killer, would have enough decency to respect such an action and feel obligated.

Yet the same man would have no compunction in shooting – or killing by any other method – someone like Belle, whom he saw as a threat to his obsession with Rawley Forbes.

Now Clint worked the overladen sorrel up through the rocks, came to a dead end almost immediately, and smothered a curse as he wrenched the animal's head round violently. The girl gave a small cry of alarm, clutched at his arm as she almost slid off the saddle.

'Sorry! Just don't want any delays.'

She said nothing but tilted her head to look into his grim, dirt-smeared face.

She saw his torment like a visible thing, at the same time hearing someone – either Hank or Forbes – cursing their mount for stumbling.

Her grip on Reid's arm tightened convulsively.

'They sound a lot closer.'

'And we're running out of rocks,' he told her briefly, nodding towards where the line of boulders, both big and small, began to show widening spaces between them, revealing the open country beyond.

A steep climb rose away from the river to the mountain trails above, offering little cover.

It was going to be a tough job for the sorrel, who was already blowing fairly hard from the desperate run that was being asked of it.

'Will . . . will we make it, Clint?'

149

He forced a grin. 'We better!'

'I know *that*. But *will* we. . . ?'

He sobered, realizing just how tense, if not down-right afraid, she must be. He answered as lightly as he could: 'Well, if you believe in crossing your fingers, Belle, now's the time to tie 'em in a knot.'

'Oh, dear!' she breathed and he felt her shoulders slump.

'We'll make it,' he added, with more confidence than he felt, especially when he glanced behind and saw the pursuers,

At the same time Hank threw his rifle to his shoulder, gripped his grey with his knees, and fired two fast shots. Dust spurted on the trail ahead, just upslope and on a line with the horse, bringing a gasp from Belle.

'Sun's in my eyes, Reid, or your body'd be rollin' downslope to me,' called Hank with a harsh, cut-off laugh. 'But I got plenty of time to sight in properly. Usin' the gal as my target. Let's see how we go this time. 'Less you wanna show some sense and stop, of course?'

Clint Reid didn't hesitate; he yanked back on the reins, Belle jarring against him, and the horse complaining as Clint swung downgrade.

'*Clint*! What're you doing?'

'Giving us a little longer to live – I hope!' He added to himself: *Can't think of anything else!*

He felt he was looking directly down what appeared to be the yawning muzzle of Hank's rifle. Forbes was a horse-length behind him and rode up alongside the eager killer, grinning tightly.

'Nice work, Hank.'

'Not – till – I – pull – the – trigger.'

'*Don't*! Or I'll blow your head off.'

Hank had been intent on his target and now jerked his head up from sighting along his rifle barrel, seeing Forbes's red, dust-grimed face, the cold black eyes boring into him.

'Aw! You're not backin' down now, Rawl?'

'No I ain't! Might look like it, but if we're gonna kill anybody, I don't want 'em found on my land.' He winked at the now slowly smiling Hank.

'I'm with you, Rawl. Where we takin' 'em?'

'Why don't we take 'em to Buckshot Ridge – the part Reid's buildin' his house on? We might even leave the bodies on that big double bed he shipped in a coupla weeks ago from Cheyenne. They say it gave the wagon driver a hernia.'

Hank roared with laughter. 'Aah, you're just too sentimental for your own good, Rawl.'

'Yeah – always been my failin'. Let's go break the news to 'em!'

They rode up the slope to where Clint and Belle had stopped on the narrow trail: this part was too steep to try to outrun the guns of these experienced killers.

So they sat there, numbed, like targets inviting the shooters to try for a bullseye.

Two bullseyes.

Forbes was tensed, his dark eyes seeming to spark with the hate – and now, the *triumph*, as he came face to face – a bare arm's length away – with the man who held his life in his hands.

'End of the trail, Reid.'

Forbes couldn't keep the elation out of his voice as he lifted his rifle.

'*No!*' cried Belle, and knocked Clint almost out of the saddle as she threw herself at Forbes, now alongside on his grey, sweating mount.

Like Clint's sorrel, the animal was quivering with the efforts and strain of the short though gruelling chase upslope. When the girl's body came hurtling towards it, it wrenched its head aside with a whinny and a snort that set Reid's sorrel edging back quickly, its rump driving into Hank's mount.

There were a few moments of wild mêlée and a gun went off – Clint's. Though the bullet harmed no one, it set all three animals jerking and snorting and trying to keep a foothold on the slope.

Clint fought the sorrel and saw that Belle had cannoned into Forbes. Arms briefly entwined, they tumbled from the saddle. Forbes's horse stumbled away, teeth gnashing in anger and fright now as it fought for balance. Forbes hit the ground first and Belle's grip gave way. She sprawled awkwardly and painfully on the slope.

Hank, face contorted, took the opportunity to snap a shot at her, even as Forbes clambered with difficulty to his feet. His Colt came up, hammer cocked, and he almost fired – point blank – into Hank, but Clint inadvertently saved the man's life by ramming his sorrel into Hank's mount. Then there was another tangle of horseflesh on the slope, Belle covering her head with her arms and screaming as stomping hoofs kicked dirt into her face.

There were two more gunshots and somehow it helped sort out the tangle, one horse – Forbes's grey – running across the slope. The girl and Clint staggered upright and he looked wildly around for a means of escape, but Forbes and Hank were too eager to keep the upper hand and he froze, one hand trying to drag the girl to her feet.

He lifted the other, looking up into Forbes's wild eyes – waiting for the bullet that would end his life.

He actually saw the whitening of the knuckle of Rawley Forbes's finger as he tightened it on the trigger. But Forbes didn't pull that last fraction that would trip the hammer: instead he smiled crookedly.

'Finish it, Rawl!' gasped Hank, getting awkwardly to his feet now.

'Ah, no! It ain't gonna be that quick for this sonuver. He's give me too damn much worry and upset too many of my plans for that. He's gonna have the pleasure of watchin' you an' me have a little fun with Miss Snippy here.' He flicked his murderous gaze to Belle, who felt the blood drain from her face. 'You like that idea, Hank?'

Hank's half-snarl – meant for some sort of smile – twisted his mouth as he said: 'Just try me.'

'Be – my – guest!'

Clint Reid stepped in front of the girl and she instinctively grabbed his left arm, fingers digging deeply into his flesh. He felt her ragged, hot breathing briefly on the side of his neck.

'Leave her be!' Clint snapped, looking from Forbes's mean face to Hank's face, which matched it perfectly. 'She's no danger to you. She saw nothing. Not like I did. I'm your eyewitness, Forbes.'

Rawley Forbes grinned tightly. 'An' don't I know it!'

'Lemme have him, Rawl,' said Hank. 'I been itchin' to put lead into him ever since he showed up.'

'Mmm. You're gonna be busy. Him *and* the gal.'

'Busy? Yeah! But a happy man. Hey, Reid. Just take a leetle step to the side, OK? Goddammit! *Move* when I tell you.'

Clint was still shielding Belle with his body, hearing her quickened breathing hissing through her nostrils now. He was about to answer Hank when she said, voice trembling:

'Clint! The money! Offer them the money.'

He stiffened, wondering what the hell she was talking about, but he saw the sudden interest in Forbes's face. Hank frowned, spoke sharply:

'Hell! She's stallin', Rawl. Don't fall for that.'

Forbes lifted a finger towards Hank without looking at him. His gaze was on the girl. Money. Now that interested him; interested him a lot right now.

'What money?' he snapped. 'Or are you just stallin' like Hank says?'

'Sure she is, Rawl—'

'No!' cut in Belle, as Clint turned his head to look at her. And he read a pleading in her eyes as she whispered so only he heard: 'Just go along with me

154

on this, Clint.'

He nodded slightly after a short pause.

'Well?' snapped Forbes impatiently. 'What – damn – money?'

She shifted her gaze to Clint, who was standing beside her now, the better to read her expression. 'The wedding money, Clint. Oh, I know you scrimped and scratched to save that eight thousand dollars but – well, it's no good to us if we're dead.'

He saw where she was going with this now.

'Goddammit, Belle! That money's for a decent house for us, and good furniture like you've always wanted. Antique if you prefer. I went hungry plenty of times just to put an extra dollar into that nest egg, and now you want to give it to these sons of bitches and—'

Just before Forbes stepped forward and clouted Clint across the head with his gun barrel, she said:

'There won't be any house, you damn fool, if you don't buy our way out of this.'

His frown deepened, and out of the corners of his eyes he saw Forbes and Hank exchange glances, both giving a brief smile: they were enjoying themselves.

And why not? They held all the aces.

'You better listen to her, Reid,' Hank said. 'She's got more brains than you.'

Clint looked squarely at Belle. 'You really think giving 'em the money'll buy us our lives? With scum like this?'

'Don't be so foolish. You – you're only making them more and more angry.'

155

'Hey, girl!' Hank said loudly. 'Just where is this money? 'Cause I tell you now, if you figure you can stall by havin' us ride into Laramie to get it from the goddamn bank you are gonna fall flat on your face – and it won't be pretty when I do let you get up.'

'Keep it up, Hank,' Forbes said quietly. 'You're doin' fine.' Then he raised his voice. 'Is that all this is? Some sort of delayin' thing to give you a chance to think up some way of gettin' outta this alive?'

'It's your only chance of you getting your hands on that much money, Forbes,' Clint told him.

'Sure,' Forbes said suddenly. 'But just how in hell could you find eight thousand bucks to put in the bank?'

'For a start it's not in any bank.'

Forbes and Hank exchanged those slow, crooked smiles again.

'Where is it, then?' Forbes snapped.

Clint deliberately looked at Belle and she tightened her lips, seemed to hesitate, then nodded.

'Show him, Clint.'

'You – sure?'

'Of course I'm sure.'

'*Show* him, she says!' Hank echoed her words, his eyes glittering. 'Now what the hell is this?'

'Dammit, Belle! Don't say no more.'

'It's way too late to try to dismiss it now. Can't you see that?'

She sounded angry and kept sweeping her gaze past him, moving her eyes towards the higher part of the slope.

156

Then she stamped her foot. 'Don't be stupid, Clint! It's our only way out now. And I remind you that I said at one time that some drifter might camp in that line shack of yours and find our . . . hoard, and *steal* it.'

'Well, you were right,' he said after a pause to catch up with what she was trying to tell him. 'Only it ain't a drifter doing the stealing. It's these two, and I can think of a lot worse than "drifter" to call *them*!'

Forbes hit him again with the gun, this time knocking his hat off. The skin broke and a trickle of blood coursed down the left side of his face. Belle stepped up close to him and steadied him as he staggered.

'Oh, Clint! I'm – I'm sorry. I didn't mean for you to get hurt.'

He shook his throbbing head sharply, rubbed at the cut, ignoring the thin stream of blood.

'It's – it's better than dyin', I guess. You were right, Belle. The money ain't important, no matter how hard it was to get together – as long as it buys us a way outta this trouble.' He turned to look at the alert killers. 'You guarantee that?'

He could see that Hank almost laughed but stopped himself just in time. But Forbes was more leery.

'You better not be pullin' somethin',' he said tightly. 'I warn you, Reid; if you are – well, they'll hear the gal screamin' down in Laramie, while you watch, tied to a tree.'

'An' when we finish with her,' put in Hank, chuckling openly now, 'we'll give all our attention to *you*.'

157

Hank was mighty eager to get started on hurting one or both of them and, while Forbes was still suspicious about this 'money', he was willing to take a chance: after all, he and Hank together could take Clint Reid and break him in two without missing a drag on their cigarettes. *Couldn't they?*

'Come on!' Forbes said suddenly. 'We already know it's hid in that line shack you're building up on the ridge. We can go an' tear it apart and find it, but why should we when we got you to just dig it up or whatever and hand it to us?'

'You always were a lazy son of a bitch, Forbes,' Clint said, and ducked quickly, anticipating the angry swipe with the gun that Forbes held.

It whistled over his head as he lunged forward, ramming into Forbes, arms going about the man's waist, but failing to pin the man's gun hand.

The Colt went off with a roar, almost but not quite drowning out Belle's sudden screams.

It turned Clint's blood cold, but he continued driving with his legs, the motion carrying him and Forbes down the slope – right into Hank.

The killer tried to dodge, but his boots slipped on some loose gravel and he went down to one knee. Clint had his hands full with the struggling Forbes now: the man was clubbing wildly with his six-gun, striking the tip of Clint's left shoulder, numbing his arm.

It fell away to his side, briefly dead, and he lifted his right arm, reaching for Forbes's throat. The man's gun came up and Clint swiftly made a grab for it. They fumbled together and there was a dull explosion, a searing pain in Clint's side, and he fell back. It was only when he hit the ground that he realized he now held the smoking gun. Forbes was down on his knees, hands clasping his face, half of which was blown away and the remains very ugly with blood and torn flesh.

Apparently the Colt's muzzle had been turned upwards when Forbes had squeezed the trigger; the muzzle flash had seared Clint, but the bullet had taken Forbes under the jaw and—

Hank almost screamed: '*Rawley*!'

Then, with a sob, he spun towards Clint, who was kicking the dead man away from him. Hank fired and Clint grunted as he felt a pile-driving blow in the chest that knocked him back violently. He fell, flat on his back, gagging, with Belle's scream ringing in his ears, and blurrily saw Hank now lifting his Colt and swiftly thumbing back the hammer for another shot.

This time aimed at his head.

Then he was almost deafened by a gun going off close to his right ear. Hank spun violently, throwing his gun away from him as a bullet slammed into him and drove him backwards. He missed his footing and began to roll down the slope . . . and roll . . . and roll and. . . . Until he brought up against a rock, his body seeming frail and broken as it curled around it.

Dazed, lying on the ground now, still short of breath, Clint clasped at the spreading pain on the left side of his chest and looked up into Belle's white face.

159

'Did – did you do that?' he gasped as he saw the smoking pistol drop from her hands.

She nodded, tears streaming down her face now. 'I – I thought he was going to kill you, and I grabbed Forbes's gun.' Then she pushed back suddenly, looking puzzledly at him. 'I . . . I thought his bullet . . . hit you in the chest?'

'It – did,' he said with a grimace. 'Feels like I've been kicked by a horse. Likely have a bruise the size of a coffee cup. See?'

He fumbled at his ragged shirtfront and showed her the mangled deputy badge, dangling by its bent pin above a spreading red area on his chest.

'This is what it hit. Didn't even penetrate the – badge. It's one of the older ones, made of heavy brass – not like those they use now, stamped outta tin plate. 'Fact, Si McLaren told me this was his very first law badge.'

'Then he left you a wonderful legacy,' she said, taking his face between her hands and kissing him soundly.

When he could catch his breath, he nodded.

'I'll go along with that. You . . . all right now?'

She shook her head and crushed herself against him causing him to grunt with pain. 'I will be! Till then . . . just hold me, Clint. Just – hold me.'

'Pleasure, ma'am,' he said, smiling, tightening his arms about her. 'My – pleasure!'